the
Song
of
Us

the Song of Us

KATE FUSSNER

 KATHERINE TEGEN BOOKS
An Imprint of HarperCollins Publishers

Katherine Tegen Books is an imprint of HarperCollins Publishers.

The Song of Us

Library of Congress Control Number: 2023930007
ISBN 978-0-06-325694-1

Typography by Kathy H. Lam
23 24 25 26 27 LBC 5 4 3 2 1

First Edition

♪

For   Clare,
who helps me write
my favorite love story
every   day
(ours)

OLIVIA

Origins

My mother liked to say,
> "You came into this world
> a game of checkers: always ready
> to leap forward, backward,
> any which way to win."

My mother liked to say,
> "You came into this world
> a scattering of Legos:
> full of both danger and potential."

My mother liked to say,
> "You came into this world
> a word search, though
> it didn't take long for you
> to find yourself."

My mother says less now that her fog returned.

> So I swap game pieces for gel pens
> trade blocks for beats
> stop searching, start writing
> the poems Mom needs
> to find her way back to me.

Now in Poetry Club

When I finish reciting
this newest poem
I glance around the classroom.

Elijah's eyebrows scrunch
like maybe he is trying to figure out
what the hell is wrong with my mom.

Lexi nods. Like always, she gets it:
I make joy Mom can't unmake in me.
Lexi got it long before seventh grade,

before she had language
for how to come out as trans,
before I had language to come out as queer,

or how to talk about Mom's mental health,
or anything more complicated
than Dora the Explorer.

Side by side since K-1
we're a couplet, stronger together.

Lexi and I started Poetry Club
as a space to hold our sounds and selves as sacred.

Elijah joined last year, and he's been mostly cool,
though he sometimes needs reminders
not to swear for the sake of a slick rhyme.

Brianna and Precious are identical twins who
occasionally bring their cousin Jennifer, but today

it's just the five of us, and it feels right to begin
the first day of school like family.

As for Me

This year I plan to
work wonders with my words
fill blank pages with verse

stun strangers with similes
turn letters into laughter

master meter

draft delight

rewrite reality into
nothing but radiance.

That is all I need.

Until *she* walks in.

New Girl

The moment New Girl walks in,
I sit on my hands, try to ignore
sweat beading between my skin and the cold metal seat.
Love at First Sight is not a thing, but
why is it suddenly hard to swallow?

                                        "Is this Poetry Club?"
You know when you first hear a song
and instantly add it to your favorite playlist?
Her voice is that. Already. On repeat.

I can't find a single word

Lexi saves me from myself.
"Welcome, come join us!
Today we're writing about family."

Lexi sets a timer for us to rewrite,
but all I do is waste time recklessly, breathlessly
wondering if it would take longer to count
the freckles on her face,
the dark brown ringlets on her head,
or the beats per minute bursting from my chest.

I scramble to scribble
but my mind says *wrong*
to every word I write

my mind says *Must look like*
I know what I'm doing.
Sit up straight. Breathe.
Find your words.

Can you fall in love
before you even learn a girl's name?
Before today, I would have said no.
After today, I have to say . . .

EDEN

Origins

Hanging out at my locker, practicing
8-24-13, 8-24-13, 8-24-13
until my fingers memorize the combo.

I skim each poster
for something to do.

It's Wednesday, the only day
Dad's shift ends early.
Anything is better
than his commanding silence
waiting for me at home.

No Music Club.
Typical.

Someday, I'll go to a school
like they have on TV,
with a band, or at least a chorus
that needs a keyboardist.

Someday, I'll channel
my talent into YouTube,
perform on a real stage
with a friend-filled audience

cheering
for me.

Someday, someone will
want what I've got.

At First Sight

I pause to read closer
a true-blue poster.

8-24-13, 8-24-13, 8-24-13

My heart switches
time signature

4/4 to 3/4

a rhythm
I don't recognize

in my typical tune

like my heart knows
something I don't.

POETRY CLUB!

Word nerds!
Phrase fabricators!
Verse nurses!

Wednesdays 3:35–4:35
Ms. G's room—129

Leave your blank pages at the door.

I can't help but smile.
Who writes like that?

But I remember, too,
my English teacher said
poetry is like music.

I may not know poems
but melodies move me.
I may not know why
but my gut says

Go.

New

"Is this Poetry Club?"

three schools in four years
two wrong classrooms
before I find 129

my question asked
in a voice so small
it might not even be mine.

I take a seat

across the circle
sits the most beautiful girl
I have ever seen.

Mermaid waves fall from her head,
brown fading into blue-dyed ends,
her hair is earth to ocean,
her eyes spring leaves.

People call this feeling butterflies
but I think it's more like hiccups,
my insides repeat
like-like   like-like   like-like

and I don't know
if I want to hold my breath,
make this feeling stop.

My cheeks burn,
stomach churns.

A beam of sunlight:
I can't look at her,
don't want to look away.

I try to distract myself

by looking at the others:

Brianna and Precious,
otherwise identical,
wear blue (Brianna)
and purple (Precious)
glasses and lipsticks and beads
at the base of their braids.

On Elijah's shirt,
lightning hits
an anime character
mirroring the bolts
shaved into his brown hair,
and his long brown legs
stretch like he's a poet by day,
superhero by night.

Last, there's Lexi, with side bangs
falling in front of her brown eyes
and a black leather jacket and white tee
making her somehow look paler
than I do, which I would say
is a feat except

right now my face
is cherry red
because no matter
how hard I try
I can't stop myself
from looking back
at Olivia.

It's not like

this feeling is new.

Like elevator music,
these feelings play
in the background

though I still can't
name the song
or the artist.

But, want to or not,
I can't ignore it.

This girl is

a power ballad:
bold, clever, all confidence
joy at full volume

a dance song: moving
words and her audience to
any beat she wants

a theme song: except
now I'm in trouble with her
stuck inside my head

*"Attention, all students,
the building is closing . . ."*

The announcement
breaks the spell
I'm under.

It's for the best.

I can't
take any of this
heart-fluttering
gut-stuttering
with me.

Instead,
I stifle this singing
silence this ringing,
know neither is welcome
in the dead air of home.

I grab my things
and go.

At the front door of my house

I seal off
any parts
of my heart
that might
still leak,

or let on
that I let
a little
of Olivia
in.

Once inside
I take off
my coat
and zip up
the scarier
parts
of me.

OLIVIA

A Blink

Eden runs out so fast
I wonder for a second
if maybe I imagined her.

I stack the chairs,
notice hers is still a little warm.

At least I know she was real.

The next morning

I brush my hair
a little extra

scrub my face
a little harder

brush my teeth
a little longer

practice in the mirror

Hi, Eden. Hey, Eden! Hi, Eden.

My book bag's packed

my favorite pens
(with spares to loan)

crisp composition books
(the best I own)

homework complete
(as best I could)

a skip in my step
(this crush feels good)

Attention

I fake cough in science.
Half the class looks at me,
but not Eden.

I fling my pencil in math,
send it across the room.
"Oops!" Nothing.

I answer every question in ELA
until Ms. Shea stops me.
"Let someone else have the floor."

I don't want the floor.
I just want Eden
to notice me.

On the way to recess

I line up behind her
(my chance!)
and the first word
falls from my lips,
a humiliating combination
of this morning's rehearsal:

"Heathen."

                                        "What?"

"Oh my gods.
I meant to say 'Hey, Eden'
and it came out all . . . I'm sorry.
Let me try again."

I take a big breath, slow down:
"Hey. Eden."

She cracks the first smile
I've seen in her all day,
a safe clicking open.
I'm in
I'm in
I'm in.

Inside/Outside

Inside I feel like sprinting
across the playground
twirling, singing
She sees me! She sees me!

Outside I stay casual, cool
walk with Eden
wait for free swings.

Lexi catches my eye
from our usual picnic bench
tilts her head like
What . . . ?

I pretend not to see
anything except
the girl in front of me.

Eden offers me an earbud,
and it's not only my ears
filled with music.

Each Day, Each Night

Each day I steal glances, moments,
try to make her laugh
and forget she ever had
a life without me.

Each night I read love poems,
write my own versions,
cover pages in hearts and verses,
forget I had a life without her, too.

EDEN

After the second Poetry Club meeting

I offer to put up chairs
to linger longer with her,
though all I can think to say is

"Sorry I didn't share much. I'm new to this."

All week I've composed reasons
to talk to her at recess,
but in Poetry Club her friends are major chords,
every note already taken,
roles assigned.

She points to the end of a table,
takes the other end.
We lift together.

"Don't apologize, Eden. I'm glad you're here."

I whisper to my knees
stop shaking
so I won't drop my end.

I whisper to my insides
hush
but they hiccup back
like-like   like-like   like-like.

When we lower the table to the floor,
Olivia looks at me.

Really
truly
looks
at
me.

The Bridge

My favorite moment
in any song

a passage from what you've known
to what you don't,

a journey, a moment of
there's-nowhere-to-go-but-here

a swelling signal that

this moment is important!

With Olivia's eyes only on me
I can't help but ask:

What key is shifting inside me?

Every other kid

seems to know already who they are.
Rainbow stickers and celebrity pictures
posted in lockers
define and declare
their future love lives
to the world.

At home, silence is safer
than the symphony of uncertainty
that plays on repeat inside me:

am I queer? bi? pan?

Since I don't know
this song inside me
I'd rather be quiet than wrong.

On the walk to the T

Olivia's arm brushes,
her pinkie grazes,
and she asks,

"Can I . . ."

pauses, takes
a brave breath

". . . hold your hand?"

and it's a bad idea
I know it.

Before today,
I'd have said,
"No."

But with no one else near,
and her hand so close,
today I let myself
say . . .

"Yes."

OLIVIA

The Frequency Illusion

You know when you learn a new word
and suddenly you hear it everywhere?

Like that word didn't exist
until you learned it but now you'll never stop
finding it at every turn?

In English, we learned
it's the frequency illusion.
For me, the word is Eden.

In math, Eden.
In science, Eden.
Everywhere, Eden.

And now, because I slipped a poem
on her desk, asked her if she'd stay
after school with me,

after school, Eden.

Eden. Eden. Eden. Eden. Eden. Eden. Eden.
Eden. Eden. Eden. Eden. Eden. Eden. Eden.
Eden. Eden. Eden. Eden. Eden. Eden. Eden.
Eden. Eden. Eden. Eden. Eden. Eden. Eden.
Eden. Eden. Eden. Eden. Eden. Eden. Eden.
Eden. Eden. Eden. Eden. Eden. Eden. Eden.
Eden. Eden. Eden. Eden. Eden. Eden. Eden.
Eden. Eden. Eden. Eden. Eden. Eden. Eden.
Eden. Eden. Eden. Eden. Eden. Eden. Eden.
Eden. Eden. Eden. Eden. Eden. Eden. Eden.
Eden. Eden. Eden. Eden. Eden. Eden. Eden.
Eden. Eden. Eden. Eden. Eden. Eden. Eden.
Eden. Eden. Eden. Eden. Eden. Eden. Eden.
Eden. Eden. Eden. Eden. Eden. Eden. Eden.
Eden. Eden. Eden. Eden. Eden. Eden. Eden.
Eden. Eden. Eden. Eden. Eden. Eden. Eden.
Eden. Eden. Eden. Eden. Eden. Eden. Eden.

I swear I once knew other words
but now I only know one.

3:29 p.m.

In sixty seconds
I can't be all
jittery hands
fumbling words
stammering out
only Eden.

In forty-five seconds
I need to find
my cool act like
I've done this before
met a girl I like
on the playground.

In twenty seconds
I need to breathe,
believe she feels
what I feel.

In ten seconds
I need to pretend
I've kissed
held hands
been cute
for loads
of girls
before.

In five seconds
I need to be
a smooth-talking
swagger-walking
version of
(always-awkward)
me.

A Brief Interlude from the Chorus

Lexi pulls me aside at my locker
before I can meet Eden outside.
"Be careful."

Precious, Elijah, and Brianna appear,
back her up and surround me.
"Yeah." "There's no room for drama in Poetry Club."
        "None."

"What drama? What are you talking about?"

Brianna rolls her eyes like dice.
"You two've been giving each other eyes." "Major eyes."
        "So gross."

Lexi acts like she already read this story last year.
"Love only leads to heartbreak." "Yeah." "Heartbreak."

"This is my club."

"Yours?" "Yours?" "Girl, no."

I hold my hands up, play defense.
"Ours. Sorry. What I mean is . . . no drama. I promise."

An army of crossed arms, solemn stares.
Lexi's glare strongest of all.
"Don't ruin us." "For a *girl*." "You don't even know."

I promise.
"No drama."

(I don't know if it's a promise I can keep.)

The truth is

I should probably listen to Lexi,

my first best friend,
who is rarely wrong,
the person I never lie to
(except maybe right now).

Instead I think about how
they all see what I see:
we haven't kissed yet,
but hold hands, swap stories,
sneak every moment we can

like hard candies from a glass dish,
sweet and solid,
swift and secretive, except
maybe Poetry Club can hear

the crinkle of us
unwrapping what we are.

EDEN

The Walk Home

Each time we hang out
I let myself feel the joy
the whole walk to the T.

Let myself record
what her hand feels like in mine.

But when I step off the T
and the doors close behind me
I leave the joy on the train,

imagine it traveling
to the next stop
without me.

In the Living Room

Dad, sunk into the beige couch,
like he's one with it.
A bag of TJ's corn chips next to him,
a sweating beer in his hand.
Not even a "hello."

On TV

I try to make nice,
sit beside him
and regret it.

Have you ever noticed
how parents can say so much
with nothing but their eyes?

How a head shake,
a long, cold silence,
a changed channel
when two men hug
in a TV commercial
says it all.

Inside Out

For every minute I spend
holding my breath
inside my house,
I gasp for every hour
out with Olivia.

She decorates notes with hearts,
ties my shoe at my locker this morning
when no one else is around,
kneels beneath me,
whispers,
"I can't let you fall."

She brushes a stray curl
back behind my ear
and I replay the moment
a new favorite verse
on repeat.

Each touch
isn't much,
is everything.

Right Side Up

After dismissal,
we perch at the top of the jungle gym
when she asks,

"Do you know how to hang upside down?"

"No,"

and I look down at the six feet? seven feet?

"And I don't think I want to."

"In third grade, Peter Peterson told me
I was too fat to hang upside down,
and I told him he could have a fat lip
if he kept talking to me like that."

I can't imagine
Olivia punching anyone,
but stop, double-check.
"Wait. Did you beat him up?"

"No."

She tucks in her shirt,
grabs hold of the bar
on either side,
and tilts all the way back
till she hangs
upside
down.

"I didn't have to,
because fatness has
nothing to do with strength
or hanging upside down."

A flushed face
a smile wide as the sky.

"Want to learn?"

How To Let Go

"Tuck your shirt,

                                        I do

grip the bar,

                                        I do

take a deep breath,

                                        I do

and lower yourself back slowly."

                                        I—

Suspended

Hand in hand

Everything upside down

one arm
outstretched

like my fingers
are on tiptoes
one hand
laced
with
hers

suspended
maybe a minute
maybe forever

we are the only right-side-up I see.

First Kiss

Against the school's mural,
the alphabet spelled out in bright-colored ASL,
my back rests against the sign for *E*.
Olivia close enough for me to ask,
"What's that scent? Perfume?"
"Soap, not perfume. I'm not fancy."

and because she's shorter than I am
I feel the warmth of her breath
float up to my nose.

My mind races with nonsense like
how she dyes the ends of her hair so blue?
where she got this denim jacket?
where she got her shoes?

all to avoid the truth:
I've never kissed anyone
and have no idea
what to do.

"I've never kissed anyone before."

I sigh hearing
our shared secret.

She laughs and I laugh
fade into awkward giggles

quieter and quieter
and then
at last

One

You only get one,

so if it's terrible,
at least it ends.

But since you only get one
I hope yours
ends like mine.

With many,
many, many,
more

beautiful,
quiet
kisses.

OLIVIA

when fog rolls in

i walk into our house   say, "hello?"   find mom
standing at the kitchen table   staring at a pile of
unopened mail at least twenty envelopes high   ignored
magazines and catalogs underneath   and it takes me
two more *hello*s for her to notice me   her eyes clear
skies   "oh, hi, honey, good day?"   and then like fog
rolling in   it returns   that lack of focus   eyes
skimming over everything   and i know anything i
say right now i'll have to repeat again because she can't
hold anything   when her mind ghosts me   us

suddenly, my news:
I have a girlfriend! And I kissed her! And I love her!

is another piece of junk mail   i swallow hard the lump
in my throat   where my soft joy once was   tell
her   "i have a lot of homework"

in my bedroom   i sit at my desk   try to focus on the
feeling of eden's lips   our noses touching   but find
myself staring at my pile of homework   remembering
what my health teacher said last year   how depression
runs in families   i want to smash my own brain
for letting that worry bury the image of kissing

eden   want to crush my mom for taking this day from
me   stealing my happiness   like she's done before
i feel tears coming   hate myself more because tears
do not belong on this perfect day   i scrunch my eyes
tighter   refuse to let them spill out   but only a
question falls in their place   this fear
Will I get lost in the fog, too?

The Next Day

I try to

                    catch Eden's eye across the room

stand near her in line
                    joke loud enough
                    to make her laugh

say something smart!
so smart! so she'll know
I'm here! I'm hers!

           offer her a pencil in math
           when I hear hers   SNAP!

      find any little reason
      to say hi and great idea
      and see you later?

                  she barely looks back
                    at me at all.

Did I do something wrong?

School Ground Rules

Side by side in the yellow plastic slide
this is our home after school each day
to fill with kisses,
stories, echoes of laughter.
                    "Can we keep us . . . between us?"

"Sure."
Anything to keep this magic.

Except I don't know how to keep this secret.
I expect my face broadcasts our love,
like I've become a human heart-eyes emoji,
my feelings have gone viral.

But she continues, asks
we keep our distance
in class and lunch,
can stay after school
but never past five.

"I hate when we say goodbye.
Can I have your number?"

> "You can text me,
> but never call."

I sense that something pulls on her,
so I don't push.

At home, I tell Dad Poetry Club is meeting daily,
working on a new project.
I tell Mom nothing.

Four days a week are for us,
this slide, and no one else.

One day a week, we attend Poetry Club,
sit on opposite sides so no one knows.

Lexi side-eyes me, doesn't trust
but doesn't push either.

Each of us walks forward,
follows the rules,
keeps it all together.

But secret or not

By the end of each day,
the classroom, the building
can't contain my joy.

Every day, every second
ticking toward 3:30 p.m.
another moment closer to

Class dismissed,
or
Go, get kissed.

EDEN

Balance

Like building a chord
this new life requires:

respecting the root,
my reliable home
not safe, but known.

If I count up a third,
keep Olivia at a distance
from my start

(and meet curfew,
erase all texts)
I compose harmony
in my heart.

Trouble

Trouble finds me

on our one-month anniversary,
the week before Halloween.
Ms. Shea assigns "random" reading groups
and I'm placed with a tight trio of girls
who are **not** to be messed with:

the last kid who did
ended up with
his locker glued shut.
The perfect crime,
untraceable, except
a too-faint-to-prove smell
of rubber cement
coming from the trio's side of the room.

I stay still at first, think
maybe if I'm a statue they won't
make me do all the work,
or worse, make fun of me.
But the girls don't buy my charade,
fold me into their group right away.

Group Work

Angelica assigns us roles
without argument from the group.
She shares her new gel pens
and we annotate
with fresh ink and ideas.

Tyra makes a quiet joke,
wonders if Ms. Shea was a kid
when these myths were written
and all four of us laugh
until Ms. Shea shoots us
a classic Teacher Look™.

Jessie keeps us on time
without acting bossy,
helps me correct my spelling
without shaming me.

We find a groove,
both time and pages pass fast
and I feel a pit in my gut form for thinking
the girls would be lazy or mean.
They're actually . . . *great*.

And by the end of class
our work is perfect,
they add me to their group text,
send me a first message.
See you at lunch?

A feeling I'd forgotten,
to be invited to sit
with a group of my own.

Before

There was once a school I knew well,
knew where every blue-tape-lined hallway led,
could always find the bathroom.

Had a friend group of my own,
a few schools ago, before I lost
halls, friends, all I knew.

There was once a mom I knew well,
before she left, taking my certain heart,
leaving just my body here.

Then

We had to move
to a smaller place
to afford the rent.
I don't like to talk about it.

Fine Enough

It's not like
I didn't have friends
at my last school.
But I was never invited to parties
hangouts
the movies.

It's not like
I minded.
I learned to lose myself in my work,
laugh a little extra loud at jokes
if they were ever told to me
look like I was fine

because I was fine.

But this new life here with Olivia
who meets me after school,
with this new group of girls
waiting for me in the cafeteria,
feels finer.

And on Thursday,
after a few days
with group work,
lunch laughs,
Jessie slips me
a secret note
and my life
feels finest.

In the cafeteria

which smells like day-old pizza
and two-day-old farts,
Olivia leads her chorus of poets
in conversation.

I sit with the girls,
try to blend in.

Jessie, whose dad drives a snowplow,
wants help picking out new shoes
for after the first big snow.

Angelica shudders.
"I hate winter. Do you know
what winter in DR is like?
Seventy-seven degrees and sunny."

Tyra is never bossy,
until she is.
"What is wrong with you all?
Talking about winter?
It's OCTOBER and
Jessie's got a party on Friday.
What are we going to wear?!"

The Problem with Halloween Costumes

Too childish
All Disney princesses
All superheroes
(except Black Panther,
maybe Catwoman?)
Firefighter
Astronaut
Ballerina

Too sexy
Sexy nurse
Sexy animal
Sexy maid
Sexy cheerleader
. . . anything with "sexy" in front of it
makes my dad rage.

Uninspired/Tired
Witch
Ghost
Doctor
Cowgirl
Frankenstein's monster
(who everyone calls Frankenstein)
Angel or devil
(who everyone calls sexy)

When they ask what I'll be

I don't tell them:

I don't have an allowance

and

my dad hates Halloween

and

I've worn the same
unicorn onesie
three years in a row.

Instead, I act excited.
"A unicorn!"

OLIVIA

Each Night

Under the covers
I read every love poem,
learn:

patterns of peril.

I study stories and songs,
ancient and new,
find:

songs of sorrow.

What is it with love
that makes people
fall:

in, down, apart?

Lies and promises unkept,
like no one looks
ahead:

I'll write us better.

Thresholds

Scooting up inside
the school-bus-yellow slide,
we lie together,
side by side,
with our feet barely reaching
the threshold to
the rest of reality.

I imagine a golden bubble
at the base of our feet
stops the world outside;
my mother's fog
and any fear I'll inherit it,
both bounce off to find
someone else to inhabit.
No fears enter here.

Kisses and giggles
and sweetness only
cross safely inside.

The Note

                    "My lips are starting to feel funny."
I lean my head on her chest
and slide my hand
into her back pocket
because I saw it on TV
and it looked like a good idea.
Except her back pocket
isn't empty.

"What's this?"

                              "Oh, it's nothing."

I start to open it.

                              "Well, not nothing!"

She whisks the note from my hand.

"What is it?"

                     "An invite, to a party. For Halloween."

"From who?"

I begin to sit up,
hit my head on the slide,
not hard, but not lightly either.

                              "Are you okay?"

She reaches for my head.
I swat a little harder
than I meant.
"Fine, fine, whose party?"

                                           "Jessie?"

she says it like a question,
and for a moment, a flash of anger.

"Is that a question or a statement?"

                                   "A statement. Jessie."

Alarm bells sound.
"Don't go."

Rumors about Jessie's Parties

1. No parents around.
2. The parties aren't even at her house!
3. Her older cousin hosts them. He's trying to become a DJ.
4. It's mostly high school kids!
5. There's drinking and . . . stuff.
6. After the party, drama *always* follows.

The problem with rumors is

My mom says it's like
throwing a fistful of
unknown seeds onto your front lawn
except some are poisonous plants
and some are sunflowers
and some are not seeds
but nails.

Spread a rumor, she says,
and know you have
to walk through it
the next time
you leave the house.

So all I say is

"I think it's a bad idea."

"You want to come with me?"

I underline
with my finger
the clear declaration:
ALL CAPS
all bold
BY INVITE ONLY.

"No. And
I don't think you should go either."

we both grow real quiet
and it feels stuffy
inside our slide

like we've entered
a sudden heat wave
but we're dressed
for late fall.

Awkward Silence

Is it ten seconds?
Ten minutes?
Ten hours?

I stare up
at the spot where
two slide parts meet:

a crack of light,
a fault line
between us,
I never noticed
beaming in.

Unsaid

"Do you want to hang out at your place sometime?"

> "We can't.
> It's small.
> Dad doesn't
> let me
> have people
> over."

Her voice shrinks with each word.
She never mentions her mom either.
I don't ask.

> "What about your place?"

I breathe in, refuse to let
reality enter our slide sanctuary,
could never let the truth in:

Mom doesn't come out of her room right now?

Dad works extra hours to ~~avoid it?~~
To ~~avoid her?~~
To avoid us.

I steady my voice
and breathe out.
"Our place is small, too."

We don't say anything
until we part.

EDEN

Friday Night

It's not sneaking out
if I'll be home
before Dad.

Chill

On the T ride
I retreat into my playlist,
shake off my nerves
pump myself up
with each new track.

My earbuds blast
new tunes in my ears
but I keep the same song
on inside my mind:

I belong here.
I will belong here.

I know the power of a chorus.
Repeat the words
to make them true.

Solo Spirit

A thumping bass,
jams I don't recognize.
A smell on the breath
of the girl who answers,
but I don't know her
or the smell by name.

Jessie appears
decked out like Shuri,
introduces me to her cousins.
"This is Eden. She's chill."

Angelica appears,
dressed in black
from head to toe
lipstick included,
backs her up.
"The chillest."

I don't know
what I've done
to earn that title,
feel silly dressed
as a unicorn
in a room full of strangers,
have never even been
to a real party before
but I take it
and a red Solo cup
filled with Coke and

I belong here.
I'll belong here.

After a few sips,
I start to believe it.

What I Remember I

In another room,
the high school kids
play their own games
leave us "babies" alone.

The couch cushions
vibrate the bass line,
the walls start to sweat
until someone yells.

"Open a window or something!"

We form a circle,
some on the couch,
some on the floor,
a bottle in the middle,
emptied earlier in the night.

The spinning,
the awkward laughter,
the way goth Angelica's face
blushes extra when the bottle
lands on her
to spend seven minutes
in the closet
kissing a boy
I don't know.

What I Remember II

Jessie makes room for me
in that circle, tells me
it is so cool
how I fit right in.

Tyra tells me
I don't have to play
but it isn't a big deal
and I'll have fun
and no one thinks
it's that serious.

Angelica laughs
when she and the boy
return to the group,
gets high fives from
the whole circle,
says I can borrow
her lip gloss
if the bottle
lands on me.

And I wanted that
something so close

I belong here.
I'll belong here.

The whole room
cheering for me.

But after

it feels like
this onesie
might
suffocate
me

and I might
hear cheers
echoes of
high fives
but I need
air and sky
and to find
the front door

Outside
the few visible stars
blur like smudges
on a notebook
like mistakes
made just once
and I hope
easy to erase
like quick
forgiveness

and Tyra says,
"You okay, girl?
It's just a game."

and I'm fine
I'm fine
but I need
to go home.

OLIVIA

Left on Read I

7:18 p.m.
My block goes all out for Halloween!
Want to come see tomorrow?

Certainty

I never have to wait long.
When we aren't together,
our fingers fly,

flickering, dancing

across the screens.
Apart, we find ourselves
together where we belong.

Left on Read II

8:22 p.m.
Three doors down,
there's a haunted house!
It's cool.

Left on Read III

8:25 p.m.
It's not like someone's house lol

just a series of tents
our neighbors string together
once a year and
everyone crawls through

the owners scratch at the sides
and play sound effects

It's fun and scary!

Left on Read IV

9:25 p.m.
But not, like, too scary.
I can protect you. ☺

Want to come?

Uncertainty

Zero new messages.
I restart my phone, just in case.

Zero new messages.
I scroll back through,
double-triple-check.

Worried I've missed something,
I think about calling her
but remember what she said:
no calling, only texting.

Zero new messages.
A new kind of holding my breath.

Saturday Afternoon

12:32 p.m.
Sorry!
Don't know how I missed this,
but I'd love to come see it.
You still free?

Relief Like

Hearing back from Eden,
it's not sighing with relief,
removing too-tight shoes,
or getting a hard test back
marked with a bright A.

It's more like spotting
a free seat on a crowded subway,
not sure if you can squeeze
between packed strangers and
make it in time and
fit between those already seated

but you do,

and take comfort that
you fit right in after all.

Halloween

I wait in my finest pirate attire,
shrugging to kids as they pass.
"No candy here."

For all the spirit on our block,
our house is haunted
by a different kind of ghost.

Magic

"Oh no, I'm not dressed
for swashbuckling."

Clad in a unicorn onesie
stained at the knee,
the hood squeezes
her locks to frame her
perfect face.

I raise my sword.
"Argh. There's a fortune out there
for the taking, but only for those
ready for the sails and the seas!"

"I'm sorry. I didn't know
I had to be a pirate."

She turns around to leave
and I worry I offended her.

"I'm kidding! Just kidding!"

and I take her hand,
give it a squeeze,
don't quite know
the look on her face
but I twirl her around
until she cracks a smile

and as I spin her around
realize I've never seen
a unicorn so magical and real.

In Line

We agree we're too old
to trick-or-treat but
not for a haunted tent adventure.

While we wait to get
the wits scared out of us,
I hang on to her pinkie,
can't wait to kiss her
when we reach the other side.

Eden is quiet. I poke her gently.

"You okay?"

She shifts her weight.

"You nervous?
We don't have to . . . We can go . . ."

A cloud hovers above us, my words
an umbrella or maybe a downpour.

"You seem out of it.
Did you not sleep enough?
You didn't text me until noon!"

I don't know what
she isn't telling me,
but it's our turn to enter.
I pay the $3 entry fee.

                    "You go first. I'll be right behind you."
Something about it
seems familiar, but
I lead us through.

Inside I

We crawl into disorienting shadows
a fog machine funnels
thick air around us
the floor damp, unsettling

owls hoot
ghosts boo

"See? It isn't that scary."

until a thunderous bang startles Eden
and she lets out a yelp.

"I'm not laughing at you, I swear!"

Inside II

We clamber over blankets
piled high in the second tent
it feels like an obstacle course
with a spirited soundtrack whispering
Turn back now
Turn back while you can
and a zombie springs up from the blankets.

After we scream, we laugh.
I reach behind to feel Eden,
squeeze her hand
but she never squeezes back.

"You good?"

A small gasp
a caught breath.

Inside III

Cotton spiderwebs
weave through the final tent,
softball-sized spiders dangle,
full-body goose bumps form
and I focus on the light ahead.

Eden's unicorn horn catches
on the tent's eave,
her hair springs out like a jack-in-the-box
announcing her exit. She brushes webs
off her locks, shoulders, and knees.

I take her in
from head to tail.

She is beautiful in every . . . wait.

Question

"Is that a hickey?"

Answer

Somewhere behind me,
a voice calls
but I block it out.

I climb the back stairs
to disappear, throw off my hat
and when my key sticks,
I can't get myself in or out.

A final plea makes me turn.

"Who was it?"

"Who was it?"

Somewhere on my block, a child wails.

And then a revelation:

"You went to that party.
That's why you didn't text back.
That's why you are tired.
That's how *this* ends?"

Trying
to
vanish
through
an
emergency
exit
without
sounding
the
alarm.

Shorter Explanation

I never drank before
and today I feel
so awful I may
never drink again.

Shortest Explanation

I hate myself for it.

On the T Ride Back

Must be something
about Halloween
because I'm not
the only person
in this car
crying.

I'm just
the only person
in this car
trying
not
to look
like it. Earbuds in,
unicorn hood pulled tight
around my hair,
show as little
of my face
as I can
to still
see
my
way
back home.

A song comes on,
and a memory
starts like
the next song
on this playlist
and I forgot
I added it
but I listen,
remember
the first time
I played
music
of
my
own.

For years I didn't know

what I saved my money for:
birthday dollars, tooth fairy coins
stuffed into my bunny bank.

My mother told me
Save it for something special.
You'll know it when you see it.
Like most things
my mother said,
it was true.

When I saw it five years ago
at a neighbor's yard sale,
I knew.

Mr. Davis's Yard Sale

stacks of books,
magazines,
well-loved stuffed animals,
a pair of glittery gold platform heels
sized for a woman
with the smallest feet,

two old TVs thicker
than I knew TVs could be,
a cardboard box
overflowing with raggedy shirts
smelling like basement,
three sad bookcases,
with three sad boxes
of paperback books,
a dollhouse,
a stack of CDs
with no way to play them,
two lunchboxes
smelling like feet,
and in the furniture section,
leaning against
a rickety table
was what I didn't know
I had waited for.

Keys

Nothing fancy,
a handful of settings,
no seat or stand.
Just a power button
to awaken
black-and-white keys
and the music in me.

"Thirty dollars? To play it on the floor?"

I didn't know what I had,
but needed to try.
I ran to my room,
smashed the bunny,
c o i n s s p i l l e d o u t e v e r y w h e r e.

(My mom scolded me later,
There's a hole underneath!
but who had time for that?)

Eighteen dollars and an eight-year-old smile
bought me the keyboard.

The internet my teacher
(YouTube has everything!)
practice after practice,
day after day,
sinking my butt
into carpet,
my hands
into keys,
molding rhythm
into my bones
infusing song
into my spirit.

Seat and Stand

Arrived later,
a gift I'd asked for,
should have felt
like a grand prize,

and did,
at first,
but it's hard now
to sit on this seat
and forget
what came next.

Mom's Last Birthday Card

Hope this seat and stand help you
make music for the world,
and joy for yourself.
I love you.
Mom

When I Get Home from Olivia's

I have no words
for how fast
we fell out of key

how off
our harmonies were

I take all my sadness,
sit at my keyboard
and play into the silence.

Six Months after the Seat Arrived

I was at school
when Mom left

for good.

A sudden vacancy
on the shoe rack
by the front door
where her shoes had lived.

I searched my room
for some sort of sign:
some explanation
of how she could
disappear without me,
vanish willingly,

solo.

I had tried to play for her,
read her face the way
my eyes learned notes,
memorizing each
until I could read
without thinking

but her expressions were
chord progressions too advanced
for my beginner hands.

A voice deep inside said,
This is bad

but I had tried to ignore it.
What does the gut know?

And After

No note,
no explanation
even from my father.

Our apartment,
room after room
of silence.

I didn't play once
for the first year
she was gone.

When I finally sat
down at my keys, a shout
from the kitchen table:

"TURN IT DOWN."
Without looking
I knew the expression he wore.

His new forever face:

like clenching his jaw
and shutting his eyes
might mute
truth.

Now

In our empty apartment
my ballads balloon,
pounding, volume
all the way up.
I had reasons,
unheard.

I would give anything
for answers of my own
but Olivia wants none I've got.

OLIVIA

Breakfast

sunday morning, i find mom washing dishes   startle
a glass right out of her hands when i enter   it shatters
with a "shit"   then a "watch your feet" except i am
wearing slippers and she is not   i am the one who
cleans while she finds a pair   the time it takes her
to find them is the same as it takes me to deal with the
mess   i don't have the energy to care.

"olivia. are you okay?"

i think she is asking me about my feet and the
glass   but she makes me sit while she pours me orange
juice   waits for me to spill whatever she reads on my
face   and i can't remember the last time she looked at
me like she sees me and wants to hear me   and i want
so badly to have my mom back from wherever depression
takes her   but i can't   i can't   i can't believe that
this will last any longer than these few minutes   and
the weight of last night   heavy and hollow inside me
is too big   too big   too big to risk   when she
can disappear into her sadness without warning.

"i had a fight with lexi, that's all."

"that's all? are you sure?"

no. "yes."

she stares into her coffee for a few seconds   or
whole minutes   every moment slow and sorrow-
filled   i'm not sure if the sorrow that hangs between
us is hers or mine   i sit on my hands   force myself
to sit here a little longer because if she does see me   if
she does hear me   then i want her to know   i
want her help   i just can't ask for it.

"olivia, middle school sucks."   i let out a tiny
laugh.   "i love you, and i've never met a problem you
can't fix . . . *as long as* you don't stand in your own way."

With Mom

For a few minutes,
I sit, eat toast,
remember what it is like
to have a mom who helps.

I don't tell her more,
but seeing her across the table,
leafing through a catalog
I remember what living looks like.

Before I return to my room,
she stops me.
"If you need to talk,
I'll listen."

Happily Never After

Sunday night, I can't sleep.
My mind

replays the evening,
a steep and tragic fall.
My mind

recounts stories I've read,
searches for clues we'd end like this

but my head is filled with
blank faces, blank pages

and a certainty
this song of sorrow isn't ours.

Instead of sleeping

I turn Mom's words
over in my head
again and again:
am I in my own way?

All I wanted was a romance for the ages,
a love story for always,
a song of us
happily-ever
forever and ever

a happily all ~~my~~ own.
a happily our own.

Like an entire library

crashing on top of me,
the weight of what I've done
hits my heart hard:

wrote what *I* wanted
instead of what was really
in the song of us

and when a single typo,
one little mark on her neck
a mistake I'm not even sure
why she made, appeared

I decided to erase us
completely, protect
myself from any
possibility of
more fog, more hurt.

What have I done?

EDEN

Monday

She tries to talk to me.
I shut that down,
slam my locker door.

Over the weekend
I transformed
into a dragon.

Practiced
a stoic stare,
grew scales.

"Olivia, I don't even know
why you'd talk to a *slut* like me.
I tried to explain,
but you wouldn't let me
say a single word."

She tries to speak again,
but I cut her off,
each word thick smoke.

"Leave.   Me.   Alone."

I sight read her eyes
to see if I've burned her.
And I have because

I breathe fire now.

A slut is a girl with

no self-respect

and   /   or

a tight top

and   /   or

bra straps showing

and   /   or

no rules

and   /   or

no feelings

and   /   or

no questions

and   /   or

all wanting

and   /   or

all power

and   /   or

no fear

and   /   or

safety

and   /   or

freedom

Playing with Fire

Jessie has an idea.
"I swiped my sister's vape pen.
Want to try it?"

Tyra nods coolly
into her book.
"What's in it?"

Relieved,
I wait for
the whispered reply.

"Strawberry kush."

Angelica wiggles
her eyebrows,
we laugh like
we all understand.

(I don't.)

Ms. Shea appears.
"Is something about this myth funny?"
(How do teachers *always* know?)

Tyra says something smart about how
these so-called heroes
make simple promises,
but never keep them
then gets us back to business
when Ms. Shea walks away
satisfied.

"After school?"

In the Custodial Closet

I laugh
because
I was told
this is funny

Isn't it?

Smoking
in
            here
all
            quiet
and
            close
binds
            me
to
            the
girls
            in
a
            new
way

                              I
                    lose
                              my
                    words
                              mis-
                    place
                              my
                    mind
                              find
                    my
                              friends

More

Not a clique
a squad
a crew
a pack

something stronger
I can't name

we head to ~~our~~ the playground,
This place feels different without . . .

stop myself, pull out my phone
to forget her, focus on
who I'll be now

a flock of parrots: a pandemonium
a slew of porcupines: a prickle
a group of rhinoceroses: a crash

"We're a Crash."
I test out the word,
like how the *shh*
feels less like silencing
more like an ocean hug.

Tyra smiles.
"A Crash."

Angelica leaps off the swing,
midair.
"A Crashhhh."

Jessie nods,
wise-like.

A Crash. That'll do.

Because Tyra Offers

I let her walk me
to the T;
she can tell
whatever
we've had
made me
woozy
and though
the giggles
come and go
the wobbles
remain steady
and I tell her
I can't remember
who I've been
but I like
who I'm becoming,
how maybe
I was always
meant for a Crash.

Tyra laughs
with,
not at,
me.

"Girl, you okay?
You're not making sense."

A Lingering Scent

"What's that smell?"

I pull myself
and a story
together

tell my father
who stands guard
by the door

like he's
gatekeeping hell

"Someone was smoking
on the train and
they didn't even do
anything about it!"

Throw my hands up
in exasperation
instead of my stomach up
in fear.

"Don't ever come in here
smelling like that again
or . . ."

and he doesn't need
to finish his threats
because they always end
with an understood
or . . .

OLIVIA

Poetry Club asks

on Wednesday,
"Where's Eden?"

I shrug,
like *it doesn't matter*,
even though
every few minutes
I glance at the door,

repeat
it doesn't matter
to convince myself
it's true.

Just in Case

I penned a poetic apology
stuffed into my notebook.

My jealous heart got
the best of us
but let it please not be
the rest of us

I wrote, rewrote pages of regrets,
emptied two pens in the process.

I clearly should have
heard you out
instead of filling us
both with doubt.

I penned so many stanzas,
none right   none enough.

After

"O, where is she really?"

Lying to Lexi,
a new habit
I've only just picked up
but can't seem
to put down,
like every surface is
too crowded
with rough drafts
of half-truths,
I can't free my hands.

"Don't know."

Impenetrable

In class, Eden ignores me.
Sits with Jessie,
swaps notes with Angelica,
shares hand cream with Tyra,
a force field of friends.

She leaves me
with nothing
but the scent of her lotion
lingering in the space
between our desks.

Problem

At our next meeting,
Elijah has a problem.
"Is it just me, or is it dead in here?"

Brianna and Precious eye me for a response,
but Lexi jumps in.

"He's right. Something's off."
Lexi looks at me.
I look away.

Everyone else starts talking at once.
"We're too small." "Unknown!" "Unappreciated."

Everyone stares at me
like I should have answers,
but I have nothing to say.

Brianna saves us.
"What about a Spoken Word Night?"

"YES, get me on that STAGE,
show 'em what I got!"
Elijah shadowboxes the sky
like this will be an all-out battle.

"But we have to make it big." "Epic?" "Legendary."

Brainstorm

Lexi stands at the board,
purple Expo in hand.
"Let's go. There are no bad ideas!"

Elijah shakes his head at me,
won't let my dumb joke go.
"Except requiring haikus for entry."

Brianna nods.
"That's a bad idea."

The group fires off real ideas,
better ones, and I turn them
over in my mind, see
seeds of possibility
sprout from soaking in
the water of our brainstorm.

By the end of the hour
we're awash in tasks.

We have a plan.

I have another.

My Plan

Poetry Club thinks
this is for all of us.

Poetry Club knows
we'll show all our talents.

Poetry Club thinks
this is a chance for us to shine.

Poetry Club knows
no truths of mine.

That night I dream

on a stage in a coffee shop
(or maybe it's a theater?)

I deliver the final poem
to a blurred audience
(of maybe my stuffed animals?)

only Eden is crisp in my vision
her arms outstretched

I perform an apology and a promise
we can write a new us together

I follow the floating final words
to greet kiss her wave to our fans

my mom and dad (and stuffed skunk?)
proud of the powerful poet I've become.

Dreams are weird, but I've never felt
more determined to make this one come true.

Pressed

Our school's too broke
to host it how we want it.
As club copresident
I scout locations,
knowing only I can find
my dream stage.

On Saturday afternoon,
I grind my way to
my fourth coffee shop
of the day, beat.

Each one has been
too small: Blue Brew Coffee with three stools
too expensive: Redeye Café with $8 for a hot chocolate
too rude: Purple Press with the mustachioed manager

dripping a fake apology
no filter.
"Sorry, we just don't *do*
that kind of thing."

Fair-Trade Café

doesn't have a colorful name
uses books as decor
tells me they don't do events for "kids"
(like it's a bad word)

"But we could make a one-time donation
if your school wants to raffle
a ten dollar gift card."

Seriously?

Threshold Café

You ever been
somewhere the first time,
thought

Why do I already know this place?

Add It Up

A platform for one,
two spotlights,
thirty seats,
one kind manager
offering Friday, February 13,
handing me a contract,
with two requirements:

$400
Our principal's signature.

Contract in Hand

The heart sings,
this is like the first day of summer,
all winning and endless possibilities.

The brain scolds,
more like the first day of school,
you want the win, do the work.

EDEN

Two Worlds

A human metronome

bouncing back and forth
between the Crash at school
and the crush of home

swinging left and right
between one me and another
neither truly mine

I barely keep
my own time.

With the Crash I

one breath stills us all

the art of tummy piles

one head on another tummy

one laugh bounces for all

With the Crash II

"Truth or dare."

"Truth."

"Who was your first kiss?"

"No, dare."

"You can't change it!"
"Yeah, you chose."
"Now spill."

"Well . . ."

"Come on, girl!"
"Spill it!"
"Yes?"

I invent a name,
a kiss, a story,

tell myself the Crash
makes me more me.

With the Crash III

At school,
I stand on a toilet seat
holding Tyra's hands

Jessie and Angelica
in the next stall

all four of us
barely breathing

waiting for someone
to finish their business
so we can go about ours.

When I hear the flush
a flash of fear

that these days
good ideas are like ghosts

hard to see
harder to hold on to

and I wonder
if in a past life

I would have said,
Maybe this is a bad idea . . .

but instead
my friends drop
a lit paper towel
into a trash can

and we run

After Class

After the fire "drill"
and the postponed math test
and the exasperated sighs
of our exhausted teacher,

Ms. G ends the class
at the bell but asks
that the four of us
stay behind.

"I can't prove anything,
don't know anything,
but don't think
I didn't notice
you weren't here
right before
the alarm sounded.
Watch yourselves."

Tyra, Jessie, Angelica bolt
as soon as Ms. G nods
but she keeps me
an extra minute.

"Do I need to worry
about you, Eden?"
Her face shows
real concern
but my spirit
fakes ease.

"No, Ms. G.
See you soon."

In the crush I

In my silent, stifled home
I spend as little time
as possible, the stiff air
unmoved
even when
I open
windows.

Every minute
inside
a moment
my life's
on mute.

In the crush II

dinner is heated up in the microwave we eat
I
of
my
did
cook
but
gave
will
time
try
we
chefs
not
cheese did not sound like a truck backing up

frozen TJ's pizza for the eighth night in a row
think
how
mom
not
often
her presence
my father the
energy reason
spare cash to
new recipes
never ate like
but dinner did
taste like cold
over my life with a beep beep beep beep beep

In the crush III

It wasn't perfect.
I knew, assumed accepted
all parents fight, right?

. . . but not all leave.

In the Underworld

I am half whole:
share what others want,
keep the rest to myself.

I am passive / bold:
say *yes sir* to my dad
say *I'm in* to the Crash

can barely remember
the parts of me I hide

I think I once said
yes to myself

but forget who that is
what I wanted
before.

OLIVIA

Money Matters

I twirl into Poetry Club
swaying the contract
in the air like a gift
from the gods.

But Lexi knocks me back to earth.
"Four hundred dollars?? Where we gonna get that?"

For once in my life
I wish my best friend,
coleader, was not so . . . right.

Whiteboard Brainstorm

~~Bake sale~~
~~Bags of candy~~
~~Friendship bracelets~~
~~Decorated bookmarks~~
~~Custom shirts~~
~~Slime~~
Poems?

No Then Yes

"Poems?"

"Poems! Like original vintage ones!"

"What?" "What?" "What?"

Brianna stands to plead her case.
"My mom has this old typewriter
because she thought it'd become
cool again. We'll write poems
and they'll look all . . . vintage."

Elijah scrunches his whole face.
"Vintage . . . poems?"

"Yes." "Yes." "Yes."

And finally, Elijah.
"Fine."

Sign Below

If straitlaced Lexi learns
we need *adult authorization* . . .
every yes will become a no

I trace the principal's signature
from an old welcome letter
still stacked on our mail table

counterfeit the bill

To Do

1. ~~Adult signature.~~
2. Raise $400.
3. Get back my girl.

EDEN

At Recess

Tyra is in a mood.
"Ugh. We must be
the *only* middle school
in America with recess."

Angelica is with her.
"In winter!
Are they trying
to kill us?"

Jessie releases breath
like we're still
in the closet smoking,
pauses and points.
"You see that?"

ORIGINAL

VINTAGE

POEM

$3

Brianna and Olivia sit on
black plastic milk crates
they wait for customers,
looking like a pair of lost
stranded strangers on an
island no one plans to visit.

The Crash lists/I listen

10 things more worth buying for $3

Takis (all chips, but mostly Takis)
Dunkies iced coffee
donut
gel pens
five-hour energy shot
hand sanitizer
breakfast sandwich
tiny Vaseline jar
all candy
any dumb app
ChapStick

In Their Laughter/In My Silence

A pinching,
like when your hand's grabbed
by a swing's chain links,
a sharp twinge
and I retrace
my thoughts
to escape
without tear

almost
let
myself
my self
my true self
my true in love self
my best self
my most dangerous self
out.

Stop.

"Anyone got gum?"

OLIVIA

Sorry Not Sorry

"I'm sorry to have to do this
but this was your first
and last day in business.
You can't sell anything
without authorization."

Ms. Shea doesn't
seem even a little apologetic,
doesn't get what
she's destroyed.

Lexi grabs my arm
because she knows
I'm about to lose it,
and mutters out a
sorry from us both.

"O, Breathe"

Lexi takes the typewriter case
before I can swing it at Elijah
who appears from the basketball court

sweating over the business
he ignored for the last twenty minutes
to play with his boys.

"What are we supposed to do?"

"Oh, now you care?"

Elijah huffs.
Lexi steps in.
"Enough."

I breathe, search for an answer,
won't stop because one adult
dares stand in my way.
"We need to move this operation underground."

The Real Problem

We only sold two poems.
Two.

We'll never make
enough at this rate.

We need to sell
something more
valuable.

Something
everyone
wants.

And if I'm in charge
of this club, this love story,
I need to be the one
who figures out what that is.

When I get home

I drop my book bag
let out a sigh so loud
it startles my mother
out of her book

and she looks at me
with a question
and furrowed brow.
"What's wrong?"

I can't tell her everything,
can't trust that she'll remember
from one day to the next,
but since I can't say nothing
I keep it brief.

"Sometimes I just don't know
the point of this Poetry Club
Lexi and I went through all
the trouble of making."

Mom pats the seat next to her,
makes me sit down.

Mom and Dad: Origins

My mother tells this story,

> When your father and I met, we didn't even live in
> the same state.
> I met him at a party in NYC.
> We exchanged numbers, pleasantries, dances.
> At the end of the night, he wanted my address.

My mother tells it slowly,

> A week later, the first letter arrived.
> On plain paper, he'd written FROM THE DESK OF,
> drawn stick figures dancing across the NYC skyline
> Underneath in a scrawled script, "Till we dance again."

My mother recites it like an ancient myth, solemn and
steady,

> Thirty-seven love letters arrived that summer
> with doodles and truths
> I didn't know one person could tell another.
> His words filled me with a wonder I'd never known.

Even with the fog sitting at a near distance, she tells me,

> *We could have stayed strangers, crossed paths once*
> *and never again had he not picked up the pen.*
> *The purest words can build new cities*
> *and birth lives we've never known.*

Priceless

In my room, I can't stop turning
Mom's story over in my mind,

know I'd pay anything
for a chance to rewrite

our love story

that no price is too high
to revise us

that words can be worth
far more than the paper
they're written on

and . . . suddenly I know what we have to do.

SOS Text

MEET ME TOMORROW
ON THE PLAYGROUND:
I HAVE A PLAN

Emergency Meeting of the Poetry Club

Now they crowd around me,
eager for instructions,

but I can't just say it,
know it won't make sense,

I need to make them *feel* it, too.

I recount Mom's story,
the postcards, the romance,
how each word brought them
closer and closer together

and Lexi (my Lexi!) nods
like she knows where I'm going
and by the end of the story
Brianna and Precious cheer
for my parents
and also for us

because we have a plan
to write words
worth every penny.

Except Elijah Doesn't Get It

"So what you're saying is . . . ?"

Brianna takes over.
"You're so dense, Elijah. She's saying
no one wants to buy our fake vintage poems
because they don't mean anything. But
if we write something *worth* buying . . ."

"Like . . . ?"

Precious brings us home.
"We write love poems, Elijah! We sell LOVE."

He strokes his imaginary beard
all smooth like
repeating slow and wise
to no one in particular.

"We sell *love*."

Love on the Market

Lexi pulls Kyle aside at recess,
like a love spy.
"Be honest. You like Kiara.
But you're never going to get her
without help. You've got no game."

Kyle flushes the same shade of red
Ms. Shea wears on her lips and teeth.
I wrap my arm all buddy-buddy around Kyle's,
he can't huff away.

"Don't be mad. We can help.
For ten dollars and your handwriting sample
we can get you Kiara."

"My handwriting sample?"

"Trust us."

Kyle digs deep in his pockets,
pulls a crumpled ten out,
looks at it before he lets go,
trusting we can make magic.

In Business

$10 = A poem and Kiara smiles wide across the room.

$10 = A poem and she asks for math help.

+ *$10 = A poem and they hold hands all the way down the hall.*

$30 = Three poems and Kyle spreads the news.

"Poetry Club will get you the girl."

By the End of Week Two

With six matches in progress
and money rolling in,
we offer to write Kyle
his next poem for free
for his advertising
but he declines.

"I got it from here."

Every poem we write
and match we make
feels less like a step
on a directionless quest,
more like a train whistle blowing,
our journey on track
and I conduct it all.

EDEN

With the Crash

When we walk
down the hallway
all arms and legs
scented like
fake strawberries,
I feel *powerful*,
selected
for a quartet
cooler than
I ever thought
I'd be.

Our teachers
remind us
way too often
middle school
is only a moment,
and I know it.

These days
won't last
for eternity.

But when else in life
will I slip out of art class
to fill a boy's locker
with fake spiders
because he called
my best friend ugly?

I try to own the chaos,
and not let it own me.

Back at Home

Dad wasn't always like this.
Grunts, nods, and silence.
We didn't always agree.

But we used to talk.

For all I know

maybe
my father's silence
always existed
and I didn't know.

Reserved for my mother
like a book on loan
from the library,

and when she returned him,
his silence became mine,
late fees and all.

On My Way Out of School

"I haven't heard you
next door at Poetry Club.
You stopped going?"

Why does Ms. Shea
suddenly care?
I run Angelica's gloss
across my lips.

"It wasn't for me."

"I'm surprised.
It sounded fun in there."

My mom would scold me
if she ever saw me roll my eyes,
but she isn't here. I make mine
wheels, burn rubber.

"It wasn't for me."

I turn to walk away
but her voice stops me.

"No problem, Eden. Let me know
if you want ideas for other activities.
Middle school can be hard.
It's also a great time
to figure out what you like,
and if it's not poetry,

what might it be?"

Her Question Stops Me

If I knew her better,
I might tell her what I want.

(Music lessons,
or better yet,
a band.

To come out,
or better yet,
a Queer Student Alliance.

To remember,
or better yet,
learn out loud
who I'm meant to be.)

Adults never keep secrets
even if they promise.

"I don't know, but I've got time."

Meeting Up with the Crash

I
let
each
footstep

toward
the
Crash

remind
me

I'm
fine.

Straight
stride

head
held
high.

Fine.

When I Do Think about Olivia

(I think about that moment
when you first tell a joke

the single second between
punch line and understanding

you don't know if the room
will fill with laughter or silence,

a faith in letting out
the realest parts of you

a trust I found
in Olivia,

but couldn't hold on to,
and now feel too far to know.

My life is already too quiet.

It's simply better not
to think of her at all.)

"Your teacher called"

might be the worst phrase
in the English language.

I stand in the doorway,
think about turning around
though I have nowhere to go.

"Oh?"

"Your work is fine, but she said
you don't seem like yourself."

I swallow, wonder
who is that anyway?

keep silent.

"I don't know
what she meant
but fix it.
Now."

I nod,
though
I don't know either,
just know
to survive
there can't
be any more
calls.

OLIVIA

The Business of Love

"What do we think Karla
really wants to hear from Jaden?"

This is the thing no one gets
about selling love poetry:
more than a matchmaker,
you become a love impersonator.

If you want a healthy business
you learn your match:

know the difference between
Karla C. and Carla G.,
know Jaden would never write haiku
but limericks will do.

Get it wrong,
rejection.
Write poems too perfect,
we raise eyebrows.

But if we Goldilocks our words and lines
love is theirs, money is mine.

Writer's Block

~~To the gorgeous girl I once called love~~

~~Dearest Eden~~

~~Ten things I'd tell you if you'd let me~~

~~Our slide, our time~~

~~Sorry sorry sorry sorry sorry~~

To Eden—Draft #1

Apologies, like sandcastles,
can tower or topple.

Permission to stoop here for a while
gather my bucket
filled with ocean tears
and make something out of nothing
with this too-dry sand?

If I were to build you an apology
one that represents
what you deserve

it'd take me a century
of digging
molding
shaping.

My apology sandcastle
would stand strong

no tide or wind
can batter it.

For you, I'd create

a monument of feelings,

a statue of sorries,

so tall

you and I could walk right inside

the doorway,

where I'd say,

I'm sorry.

I love you.

And I always will.

Ugh I

See? Needs rewriting.

Like eating a whole
bag of Skittles at once, too
sweet

but it's hard not to hide behind
extended metaphors, to say
what I mean:

Damn. I messed us up.

EDEN

I don't think about Olivia

(No, really, I don't.)

In Angelica's room,
we decorate canvas shoes.

Angelica squeezes the fabric paint
and the sound of the bottle farting
sends us spiraling.

Jessie holds my shoe,
my foot still inside.

"Stop pulling so hard!"

"If you'd let me paint your shoe
without your foot in it,
I wouldn't have to."

No one likes a girl with stinky feet.
But I don't say that.

The Party

ding   ding   ding

Jessie drops my foot

"Ow. Warn me!"

ding   ding   ding

she picks up her phone

"My cousin's throwing a party tonight!"

ding   ding   ding

Angelica groans about the cold

"Whatever. Wear a coat."

ding   ding   ding

a flurry of texts

"let's gooooo"

ding   ding   ding

I don't say anything

I don't need to

the Crash has spoken

We're going.

At Dinner

Angelica's family serves home-cooked food
warming me with comfort and jealousy

there is nothing home-like
about my father's cooking:
frozen pizzas from work

"What are you proud of today?"
Angelica's mother demands
we name our accomplishments

there is nothing home-like
about my father's dinner chats:
stilted at best, silent most often

here, pulled pork and celebrated spirits:
this is not what I know of family.

When it's my turn to share

my mind and plate are empty.

Angelica's mother puts down her fork.
"Every day, it's your job
to do something great.
What did you do today?"

I don't know where my tears are coming from,
want to blame it on the spice in the rice
or the speed I ate it,
but that's not it.

I excuse myself from the table,
hide in the bathroom,
wait for the Crash
to check on me.

They don't.

Cold water never helps

but I splash it on my face,
try to shock sadness out of me

the sliver of soap
melts into pieces
in my palms as I lather,
molding it toward
disappearance

I play with the bubbles,
shifting, expanding, popping,
see my fragile reflection,
nearly thin as air

wonder how far
to separate
my hands
before I
burst

Before I head home

I tell the Crash
I'm suddenly sick

spend the night
at my keyboard

learn a new song
just for me

I can't spend
another evening

pressing my body
against a random boy

pressing myself
into some pretend thing

When the Crash Is Out Partying

My voice never carries
the power my hands do,
so I let them dance
across the keys
on their own.

I start quiet,
let the day loose,
let my hands grow louder
until I feel lost
in music
instead of
myself.

This music isn't genius or talent.
Like a puzzle,
it's the work I've put in
one piece at a time.

Some kids dream of recitals,
earning scholarships,
starring in their own shows,
making themselves names
for everyone to know.

I am not those kids,
want to be a part of something
but don't need to be the star.

This keyboard is mine alone,
the only place always my own.

OLIVIA

Business Booms

In a matter of weeks
we've made two hundred dollars,
the fruits of our labors
all over the playground:

recess is no basketball
all courting.

It's a good problem to have but

"We are running out of couples."
Everywhere we look are doubles.

Too good at seventh grade
we need to expand our range

but eighth graders intimidate
sixth graders act too young to date

new markets take time to learn
too long for cash we need to earn

I have to remind our crew,
"It's good to woo as well as we do."

home is another story

mom's fog is thicker than ever   our house dry of
conversation   just the constant buzzing of the tv
behind her bedroom door   replaying old shows so
quietly   i'm not even sure she could hear it   if she
wanted to

i try to let none of mom's sadness hit me
directly   pretend it's a mist, a temporary
fog,   not a flood   but i can't ignore the signs of
water   belly-high   and my normal escape plans

(reading my poems to her, bringing dinner to her room,
gently reminding her that she always feels a little better
when she showers, telling her that i love her)

work like lifeboats with holes,
sinking slow at first and then faster
         and faster
                  until i worry that i will end up
                           underwater with her
                                    except

there are moments when it seems to work: a moment
when a glimmer behind her eye means she is still here
and she can see me for an instant before we return to
her regularly scheduled program of falling apart and i
try to remember what it is like in this house when my
mom is okay but most of the time

we wear life jackets   tread water   remind ourselves:
    even if we have to float, at least we still see the sky.

Opportunity Knocks

At lunch, Eden's new friend Tyra
holds out a clipboard.
"You guys want a dance, right.
Sign here."

It's funny how she doesn't say it
like a question,
like there's only one answer.

We sign her petition,
but when she walks away,
I speak my mind.
"Who wants to dance *in front of teachers?* Ugh.
Also I'm a terrible dancer."

Elijah chokes a little bit on his milk.
"A white girl a terrible dancer? Nooooo."

The chorus laughs ~~at~~ with me.

Lexi backs me up.
"Everything about a dance seems gross."

Elijah puts down his fork,
folds his hands together, all serious.
"Or . . . an opportunity."

"What are you talking about?"

"What if we expanded our services? Made sure
that our poems weren't just winning hearts
but also winning dates to the dance?"

I hate to be the first to admit it but I have to.
"Damn, Elijah, that's a good idea."

EDEN

Tyra's Plan

Tyra insists this isn't about her.
"This dance is for everyone's benefit!"

But ever since Saturday's party,
where Tyra and Scott Quiroz
spent a lot of time . . . talking,
she hasn't shut up about it.

Her petition makes promises
no one bothers to read,
like only students with
great attendance
great grades
can go,
because
these are promises
she and Scott can both keep.

But this isn't about that.
Tyra swears.

Would You Rather

Slow Dance with
(circle one)

Eliot E. or Elijah W.?
Danny H. or Manny H.?
Jeffrey M. or Jeremy N.?
Scott Q. (7th) or Scott Q. (8th)?

Unseen

In class, Tyra passes
around a note,
a list of only boys,
asks us each to circle our choices,
a simple game of
Would You Rather

an *it's-not-that-serious*
reminder that
not now in math
or at lunch,
when we hang out
or group-text till midnight,
do the Crash
ever see

the real me.

I Don't Know How to Answer I

because
the last question
seems like a trick:

Tyra is crushing
hard on Scott Q.
in eighth grade . . .

am I supposed to agree
with her that he's cute
or not because
she wants him for herself?!

I Don't Know How to Answer II

because
when I look
across the room

see Olivia
scribbling poems
in her notebook
instead of
solving for x

I know
we once felt
like the solution
to everything

and my friends
know nothing
about that

and my friends
know nothing
about that
part of me

and my friends
know nothing
about me

and neither do I.

OLIVIA

Expanding

With the date of the dance official,
two weeks before our Spoken Word Night,
someone spreads a rumor.

"You shouldn't even bother going
if you don't have a date"

and I'm not saying that we spread it
but I'm not saying that we stop it either.

That Look

You can see it on their faces,
the kids who hadn't thought
for even one second
that a *date* would be necessary.

The way they dive to the bottom
of the backpack, scour through
forgotten pencils, crunched homework,
pull up a ten dollar bill that smells like erasers,
say, *Please.*

We are back in business.

My Match

Do I think about asking Eden to the dance?
Every minute of every day.

Do I know better?
Most minutes of most days.

Have I written poems to ask her to the dance?
Dozens.

Have I given her any?
None.

Am I wasting my best words on matching other kids?
No words are wasted
when every dollar earned
brings me closer to her.

For Now

We've moved beyond that awkward point
where we couldn't even look at each other.

We can nod to each other,
don't argue if a teacher
pairs us up for an activity.

There is no warmth,
no familiarity no
sense of who we were.

Like our story's written in invisible ink,
our bodies here, but our spirits gone,
we act like nothing ever happened at all.

It's Almost Worse

That widened gap,
like a whole playground
and love story vanished.

To Eden: Draft #2: Apology

I read once that the word *apology*
has a surprising etymology.
It was a justification, a sort of proof
the *why* not the guilt behind the goof.

Shakespeare's to blame for how we know it
the inventor of words, from *swagger* to *bandit*.
He didn't invent apology, but he redefined
what it was and left that behind.

If I could, I'd take what I did to you
and leave it behind too.
Start anew,
for you.

I'd listen better, try to grow
let all the petty parts of me go.
I'd act with trust
for our love that is a must . . .

Ugh II

I don't know what it is I need to say
to win her back
but I've proven to myself
rhyme isn't it.

I Can't Help Myself

Right at dismissal
for winter break,
as the hallways flood
then empty,

I know I shouldn't,
but I slip Eden a note
that is not a poem
or an ask to the dance
or even much of anything

because thinking about her
steals my best words.

But I need to break the ice.

Have a great vacation, Eden. ☺

EDEN

Offerings

I hate winter break:

nowhere to go,
no parties,
trips,
family traditions.

A lot of stillness
I try to replace
with my keyboard
and YouTube.
Usually.

This year, I walk home from school
with three notes:

Jessie asks if I want her to dye my hair
Angelica asks to spend First Night together

and

Olivia, not offering anything
but an opening.

Each note softens the pit
where my feelings live,
fills the week
with possibilities.

New Year, New Me

```
I've                        But
al    might                 when
ways    change              I
hated    us                 drape
that        auto            myself
say            matic        over
ing              ally       the
like              which     edge
the                it       of
change                does  Jessie's
of                    not   bath
year                 ever.  tub
```

with pink dye bleeding from my
cold
soak
ed
hair
and Jessie tells me
I
look
fierce
and
also
hold still until the water runs clear

    some   me.
     new   new
      thing   brand
      clicks   a
        in   start   of
       side   can a   start
       of   day new   the
      me   any   year   be
        I   be   may   can
    can't May   be   day
     ignore.   any

But as soon as I get home

my father has more words for me
than he has had in months.
"What the hell did you do to your hair?"

Three washes or so
and there'll be no trace
but he doesn't care.

"I don't know
what you think
you're doing,
changing your body,
who you think
you're becoming,
acting so . . ."

and his silence
sounds like disgust.

"You need
to turn yourself
around now

or else."

Light Wishes

The only part of
Christmas Day
I ever really liked
was when my father went
to evening church
without us,

my mother
turned on tree lights
she lay
on the long couch,
I on the short
separate but together
our own kind of communion
Dad didn't understand.

We'd make wishes aloud

for every tree light
and fall asleep there

snow weighing down trees
carols lightening the air.

"The stores all play
these songs to death."

At home,
we didn't listen to them

except on Christmas
when we'd lie there
dreaming
aloud

together.

December 25

My father goes to church
without me.

I plug in the lights
on the tabletop tree
my father's boss gave him.

I keep my wishes to myself.

OLIVIA

On Christmas morning

Dad makes pancakes
and the air fills
with butter, maple syrup,
and a pine-scented candle Mom lit.

The piles of presents
waiting are smaller
than they used to be
(or maybe I am bigger
than I used to be)

but what I wanted most is there:

seven mini notebooks,
one for each color of the rainbow.
I run my hand along the soft covers
the pages and my fingers ready

and after my *thank you thank you thank you*
and *merry merry merry* I stand
to go draft something new, alone.

"Wait, Olivia. One more thing."

A hidden present

I somehow missed
and what surprises me
most is the smile Mom wears
as she hands it to me.

(I had forgotten how she presses
her tongue behind her teeth
when she manages
a real real smile and
it's not like a gritted-teeth emoji,
more like flowers pressing up
through frozen earth

and maybe that is the hidden gift.)

Under the Wrapping Paper

I unwrap a book,
heavy as a textbook
but it's filled with classic tragedies,
illustrated and retold, titled,

We Never Learn.

Mom hates the title.
"I don't agree. Sometimes we do learn.
And sometimes stories deserve repeating.
Someday we might get it right."

She leaves me with my new books
to read and to write, and I spend hours
getting lost in both and when I emerge
to recite some new verses to her

the flowers behind her smile are now covered in frost

        and i don't know   what changed

but i know

          she's gone   again.

EDEN

I've lived my whole life in Boston
but never gone to First Night.

Before Mom left,
we celebrated New Year's Eve
with my three aunts
who'd show up for New Year's
from out of state, but never
visit otherwise.

Each of Mom's sisters
stood just a little taller,
a little bolder than her
and maybe she noticed that,
because she wore high heels
when they came around.

I don't know what makes me remember
the four of them
standing in front of the couch,
posing for a family photo,

but I'm brought back to reality
when I step off the train,
see an ice sculpture of a penguin,
see Angelica

and remember that in the now,
for everything I have lost,
I've found new friends,
new places.

I stand a little straighter
to greet Angelica
and a new adventure.

NYE II

"Winter is so unforgiving."
I zip my jacket
up my neck.

"If you were an ice sculpture,
do you think you'd be a penguin?"

"I don't think I'd want
to be a penguin *or* an ice sculpture.
I hate being cold."

Angelica grabs my arm,
walks me across the street
to five more ice sculptures,
guides me from one to another.

She's soft with me
I try to loosen my knots.
"Okay, listen, if I had to be an ice sculpture,
I'd want to be an ice fox, but, like, enormous."

"That's random!"

"Your question was random!"

She points to prove
her question clearly came
from somewhere.

But I like that maybe
this is what real friendship looks like:

permission to be random.

Angelica Is Not Smooth or Subtle

"Who do you want to go to the dance with?"

"Um, again, random."

"Get used to it. Now tell me."

"No one."

She drops my arm in disbelief.
"Really? There's *no* boy? . . . Or girl!
I don't discriminate."

There's a tone

some people use
when they say

I'm really open
I don't discriminate
I accept anything

but they don't expect
anything but "normal"

add the rest of us in
as an afterthought.

They know they should
appear open but
their tone, their minds are closed.

"Really."

Maybe it wouldn't be so bad
to be an ice sculpture here.
To fit easily into the season,

cut cleanly, clearly,
lit by colorful lights

celebrated by passersby,
a strong striking statue
centered

if only for a few weeks.

A giant fox
on a city block.

Both strange and delightful,
and exactly what it looks like:
water, solid, strength.

See-through. No one
wonders what it hides.

Frozen

"But I've changed my mind
about being an ice sculpture.
I think I'd love it.
And I would definitely be a fox."

Open

Is it from the
frigid night air?

The fireworks we saw?

A sudden belief
a new year
can start
everything
fresh?

I don't know.

But something in me
cracks open a little
when I see texts
from Olivia
right after
midnight.

It Says/It Doesn't Say

Hey. Happy New Year!

So I'm planning a thing
(a Poetry Night) in February.

It's Top Secret right now,
Please don't say anything to anyone!

It means everything to me.
Would you come?

An urgency
I don't know what to do with.

"Okay."

OLIVIA

An Opening

Okay is a window,
clinging to the frame
until a pressured pull
releases a sunny sigh.

Okay is a match tip
snapping alive.

Okay is the hiss
of twisting a plastic soda bottle cap,
that first carbon sigh
sweet tingling bubbles dancing.

Okay is less than a promise,
more than a wish.

A Brief Interlude from the Chorus II

On the first day back,
I call an Emergency Meeting.

"We have eight school days until the dance,
seventy dollars to go. We can do this!"

"Relax, we still have a few weeks."

"Don't tell me to relax, Lexi.
How else will I make the money
after this stupid dance?"

"Will *you* make the money?
Right, this is all about *you*.
We're just your minions,
you don't need us."

This kindling will become a full-blown
friendship forest fire
if I don't extinguish the problem now. "Sorry.
That's not what I meant."

Embers hiss.
Everyone watches   waits.

One Final Order

"Tell me what this is really about."

"What?"

"Why do you want this Poetry Night so bad?"

"I . . ."

"Don't lie to me. Something's up.
You've never cared about the club
becoming popular, or anything more than
spending time together writing. Since
we decided to do this, it's the *only*
thing you care about."

"I . . ."

"Tell me."

So I Do

Like a broken gumball machine,
once I start spilling I can't stop.

                              the yellow slide

                    the first kiss

    more kisses

            the all-night texting

                        the fight
                              the loss

            the lie to Mom   and
                        Mom's sadness

All the pieces of me roll across the floor
wait to slip me up everywhere I walk
so I don't move.
The Poetry Club witnesses my whole unraveling,
but I focus on Lexi,
who listens, holds my hand.

Finally Empty

Lexi proves
for the thousandth time

why she's the best friend
I've always needed.

"Let's get this money,
and get *you* the girl."

Orders

Elijah returns from the boys' bathroom
victorious, holding up fifty dollars.
"I told the boys that if they want dates
they better get on it!"

He hands me the cash and
a scribbled list of names on a Post-it note
written in the crappiest blue ink
I've ever seen.

"Elijah, I can't even read this."

"I had to lean up against the bathroom wall!"

"Then use a pencil!"

He starts to rewrite it
and his face scrunches
at his own scrawl.

"See? Unreadable."

"Nah, I got it."
He hands me the rewrite.

Brianna returns from the girls' bathroom
with two more requests,
and we have what we need.

The last orders,
the final steps
between here and home.
We are so close.

Volunteer

I feel powerful, filled with creative energy
so close to our goal.
"I'll take care of the writing tonight,
and you all deliver tomorrow."

"Can you have those all done by tomorrow?
That's a lot of poems in one night."

I nod, know
I'll be up late
fulfilling orders
for other people's crushes   for my own dreams.

When the world falls out from under you

the ground gets farther and farther away looks
something like this:

you come home from school to write love poems find
your mother sitting in the hallway   linen closet door
open   soaps and boxes of contact lenses   band-aid
tins and lotions on the floor you go to her   kneel take
her hands try to help her up   she is too exhausted from
crying to get up
                    yet

so you sit with her   try to remember that this isn't *her*
that it's like your teacher said some sort of broken path
in her brain   or a series of cracks in her mind but this is
not *her* and this is also not you

when the world falls out from under you   you convince
yourself that what she says right now
            she doesn't want to exist or in this world isn't
            about you or your presence in her world   but a
            mind trick   a mind trap

you close your eyes for a second   set a mind trap of your
own

imagine a warm glow around
you   protecting you

from holding on to now a single second longer
than you need

you stand up   pull her up with you   guide her to bed

text dad *help*   make her tea   hope she falls asleep
before the kettle whistles

lie on the bed next to her
watch the tea's steam rise,
disappear
remind yourself when the
ground returns
the world still spins
and you have words to
write.

It Takes Me All Night

Seven love poems
take seven hours,

longer than I thought
but I spend time

staring, listening.

Any sound might
be Mom stirring,

but everything is settling.
My father gets home,

there's whispering,
more tea made,

Dad leaves a voice mail,
the bedroom door closes.

Finally, the apartment
and my mind quiet

I'm able to craft love
notes I need,

fold each into an envelope,
seal with names and heart stickers.

If I can lead others to the dance
I can lead Eden back home to me.

EDEN

An Invitation

Tyra throws her bag on the lunch table.
"I have to tell you guys something!"

She runs off to get lunch,
returns out of breath.
"LOOK!"

She holds up a letter—
no, a love poem, that ends

Will you save a dance for me?

Angelica's eyes go wide.
Jessie holds up a high five.
Together we raise our milks
to Tyra and Scott.

"What will I wear?
What will we dance to?
Will we have, like,
a song that's ours?!
How will I know which it is?"

I zone out,
care so little
about the questions
and answers.

Every other kid II

seems excited about the dance.
New outfits and personal invites
define and declare
their current love lives
to the world.

I know better
than to get carried away,
know I can't even go
with Olivia if I wanted to.

I'm not saying I do.

But

since the dance doesn't mean to me
what it means to everyone else,
I quiet myself this time.

One Minute

The night before the dance
I allow myself one minute:

eyes closed
sixty seconds
a vision of us

not yet moving
not yet holding

but standing
together

and the question
I want to hear

sits on her lips
the words rise

from her lips to mine
Want to dance?

a vision of us
sixty seconds
open again.

What We Will Not Remember from Olympus Middle School's Only Dance

Knock-off Oreos

7th grade math teacher "DJ Pi"
in a rainbow clown wig

a dance circle
around three 8th-grade boys
showing off moves
like they rehearsed
for this movie moment

our school mascot
joining them
with the Panther Prowl,

a cheesy move
that will not go viral
no matter how hard
our teachers try,

the speech by Principal Z
welcoming us to this dance,

a special achievement
for all those who
"Work Hard
Be Kind
and Show
our Panther Pride"

What We Will Remember from Olympus Middle School's Only Dance

When Tyra spots Tiara
chatting up Scott

time gets real slow
anger comes real fast

fifteen fury-filled steps
one "Excuse me?"

shouting starts
shoving next

and Scott
does *nothing*

(might even like it?)
(even if he doesn't get it?)

until Tyra and Tiara pull out
love poems in identical envelopes
both from Scott

and 7th grader Scott Quintanilla
steps forward

"There's been a mistake."
He'd written to Tiara

but still it takes another
two whole minutes

to calm the gym
into silence.

"Who is responsible for this?"

The classic Teacher Look™
from *all* teachers
simultaneously
reading our faces.

Elijah, Lexi, Brianna, and Precious
try not to look at Olivia,
but fail all at once.

She stammers
in front of everyone.

"Wait, this wasn't just me!"

OLIVIA

Shame

I wait to learn my fate.

My classmates walk back to class,
whispering as they pass.

"That's rough . . ."
"Yo . . ."
"Wouldn't want to be her."

Tyra and Tiara
sit in opposite lobby corners,
won't even look at me.

I don't blame them.

I don't blame Lexi,
or the others either.

I pushed for this.
I needed this most.

The fault is mine.

Tiara is called in first,
gives me time to plan
how to explain
what this is all about,

but I can't find words.

Only shame.

In walks

my mother
through the front door
dressed (not

in pajamas
or a bathrobe

but) the part,
dark slacks, thick sweater,

professional,
in charge.

I almost don't recognize her,
distrust she's real.

Lies I Could Tell My Mom

I was framed

there's been a mistake

I didn't have anything
to do with this

it was all Elijah's fault

I don't even know
anyone named Tyra

Some eighth grader
blackmailed me
to write love poems
and I . . .

I have no idea

When You Need a Champion

The truth unfolds like a red carpet of honesty,
rolled out right there in the main office:

how I loved and lost so quickly
turned my art into a business
forged the principal's signature

how I am so close
the money is made
I can't accept defeat

how now I fight *for* Eden instead of *with* her
learn from every poem I write
every vision I have of this night

"Mom, I could really use your help."

Three Things Everyone Knows about Principal Z

1.
her daily greeting
a sharp suit on the front steps
our school's rain or shine

2.
like invisible
magnets, her hands attract phones
repel objections

3.
when students or staff
get called to the main office
none return the same

Now

"I don't want an excuse.
I want an explanation
for what this mess is
and how you intend to fix it."

I fumble every word until

my mom starts,
"Excuse me, Ms. Z—"

"Dr."

"Dr. My apologies.
Is that your wife?"

Mom points to a framed photo
on the bookcase above her

two Black women
facing each other

all joy

a candid capture of
love mid-laugh

And I can't believe what I see

Dr. Z smiles.

I don't know what Mom's goal is

"That's a lovely photo and also inspiring.
To see such love and such leadership
at the helm of this school.

This is what I want for my child:
to see that everyone deserves love,
strength, compassion.

I don't think that's far
from what Olivia wants, either.

Didn't you ever do anything
a little daring for love?"

Instead of waiting for her response
Mom looks to me.

"Mom, I can't—"

She shakes her head,
lifts her hand
signals

Speak.

If You Can Believe It

It is possible to find love at thirteen.
To see in the eyes
of another
a different
kind of home.

It is possible to find love at thirteen.
To know it in the words
in the laughter
in the comforting silence
of another
a different
kind of peace.

It is possible to find love at thirteen.
To feel it
linger by a locker
a drive toward tenderness,
even if we're too young
to have licenses.

It is also possible to lose love at thirteen,
a fact no one argues
even if they'll say all night long

that true love can't be known this young,
they'll say it sure can be lost.

It is possible to find forgiveness, to forge a love anew,
To build a new life together,
to try again at thirteen,
to say
I was wrong
and
I know better now
and
I made this all for you.

That Was All I Tried to Do

"Fix a mistake.

I'm sorry,
I really am.

Give me detention!
Make me clean classrooms!
I'll do it every day for weeks!
I'll apologize to everyone!

Just don't cancel our night.
I need to get her back.

Please."

For the longest time

no one speaks.

Three Stares

Mom at the photo

me at the floor

Dr. Z at me

Silence so long

I can't tell

if it's good

or bad

or the worst

Finally

"You may have your Poetry Night
on three conditions.

But if you mess up on *any* of these rules,
I'll disband your club

forever

and you'll serve
detention every day
for the remainder
of seventh grade."

Conditions

"1. Two weeks of cleaning tables after school.

2. Make amends.

3. Find a teacher chaperone willing to supervise from start to finish. If either of you step a toe outside the café before it is spotless, goodbye Poetry Club, hello detention."

When I leave the office

Tyra's mother in green scrubs
does that thing moms do so well:
whispering *and* yelling simultaneously

Lexi and Elijah each hold a bathroom pass
sneaking out of class to check on me.

I have all these sorrys to say,
a teacher to find
a night to plan

but all I want is
to hug my mom.

EDEN

Lunch with the Crash

"Two weeks of detention
for some shit
I didn't even start!
When can I hang with Scott now?"

Tyra pushes around
mac & cheese like
she's mad at it.
A fleck of cheese flies.

"Ew, Tyra, chill.
Scott's not going anywhere."

"Yeah, girl,
take some deep breaths.
He *likes* you, remember?"

Jessie and Angelica
voices of reason,
my voice
nowhere to be found.

"Tyra?"

Apologies

Olivia takes a huge breath
like she's about to be plunged
and held underwater.

"I'm sorry.
It was my fault
the poems got mixed up
and—"

"Save it."
Tyra's voice is stone.
"I have detention
because you're a dumb b—"

"Tyra, stop!"
She is as startled
by my voice as I am.
"You don't need
to get in more trouble
for swearing at her and"
I don't even think as I say it:

"People make mistakes
and they get to say sorry."

Break

everyone waits
to see if Tyra
will chill.

"Whatever."

She grabs her still-full tray,
throws it in the trash and leaves.

A crack in the Crash

visible now
not new but

too wide to ignore.

Before she leaves

Olivia mouths
a silent

thanks

I wonder
if she knew
what I meant.

You can say sorry.

After School

I lose myself
on my piano bench

fill the apartment
with song

sit so long
my legs fall asleep

mind so full
with the day and how

I keep hitting
the wrong note

in relationships
and myself.

Late That Night

My phone glows yellow
and I should ignore it,
should get some sleep,
but texts I didn't expect
cut through the shadows.

*Thank you for
standing up for me.*

    and

I owe you an apology.

    and

*I should have given you
the time, the space to speak.
I'm sorry.*

Because it's Olivia
I expect an ellipsis
a sign she has more
to say, to send.

But now it seems
she waits for me.

Don't Look Back

In the glow of my phone,
I transform

dragon
to ice fox

The gut says,
I want I want I want.
I can't I can't I can't.

I won't stay frozen
but maybe, maybe
if I warm so slowly
I can phase forward

be water
flow toward
who I could be.

Replies

You are right.
You were wrong.

Can you forgive me?
Can we be friends again?

One step
at a time.

In the Moments After

When I text
I need sleep

she asks for just
one minute more

explains her vision
for Poetry Night

she's planned
for me

and no one has
ever offered such

a lovely gift
but I hesitate

yes or no
too much like promises.

Maybe.
Good night.

OLIVIA

Maybe

A maybe is
drawing back curtains
to let in light

an open book quiz,
a lottery ticket.

I can live with maybe.

Math Problem

"A Friday night?
That's a big ask, Olivia.
What's in it for me?"

I look around Ms. Gonzalez's room
note random papers scattered
lost pencils discarded on the floor.

"Could you use a personal assistant?"

"If you can solve this:

Olivia needs four hours of help for an event she's planned.
She's offered to pay her teacher back in time by helping out
organizing her classroom before school. If Olivia organizes
every Monday for one hour, how many weeks will it take for
her to repay her favorite math teacher of all time?"

Ms. G is so cheesy,
but also I need her.
"Four."

"Correct. Do we have a deal?"

Morning organizing.
Afternoon cleaning.

My days fill up
but the only path is forward.
I can't stop now.

Countdown

In ten days
I can't be all
shaky legs onstage,
stammering for any word
other than Eden.

In eight days
I need to find
my poem, act like
these words flowed out
effortlessly
for a girl I loved
on the playground.

In six days
I need to breathe
believe
she feels
what I'm feeling.

In four days
I need to act
like I've declared
my love,
been the hero
of a love
story
before.

Draft #3

I have learned more without you
than I thought was possible,
learned wrong and right
how it can be impossible
to tell the difference.

I have learned more without you
than I thought was possible,
learned my heart is bigger
my words are weaker
if they aren't going
straight from my heart
to you.

I have learned more without you
than I thought was possible,
my body is stronger
my wit is wiser,
my plans can be met
if I work toward them
and nothing else.

But what I have learned most without you
is that I am better with you.
That I will be better with you
if you'll let me.

Our love was brief
but changed me forever
and if you'll have me
you'll never wonder
if I won't listen to you.
I will.

Because all of this
is for you.
All of me
has always been
for you.

Ugh III

But every time
I sit to write
it's sappy crap
keeping me up all night,

Sappy stanzas spill from my pen,
more determined than ever.
But performing this mush?
I could never.

A Glimmer

A little flirtation
no more than a glimmer

in every text I send
and receive

first a

Maybe

then

Cute shirt today ☺

I don't know how to not come on strong
because all I want to say is

~~Promise me you'll attend Poetry Night~~
~~Promise me you'll let me show you~~
~~how sorry I am that I ever let you go~~

but that is a bad idea.

Thank you. ☺

I am spring-loaded,
need to believe

my work will pay off
but I have to let her
write her own way
back to me, too.

So this glimmer will have to do.

EDEN

Tyra is still mad at me

Jessie and Angelica
try to keep peace

at Tyra's apartment
we paint our nails neon pink

stinging my eyes:
the smell of nail polish remover
Tyra's glare

Interrupted by two texts

Jessie's phone
announces
another party
Friday night

my phone
Olivia says
hi

both messages
vacuum up
all the air in the room

I don't know how
to hold both things

separate but together:

the Crash   Olivia

I don't know how
to hold myself

separate   together

Jessie decides

we should meet before

the party to get dressed together

make a whole night out of it

except

it is the night of Olivia's poetry event

except

these parties
where we sip nips

kiss boys we barely know

like roller coasters

I always think I like a thrill

until I ride

and my stomach flips

"It's going to be *everything*"

and since the Crash declares it

I paint excitement on my face

don't know how to say no

don't know if I want to

or what I want.

After all

I owe them

new girl
no friends
dumped

welcomed in
to parties
homes
group threads

and I think of
rubber cement
fake spiders
what else
they might try
if I say *no*

and I remind myself
isn't this what I wanted?
A Crash of my own.

But

no one tells you what to do
when friendships change
or when people do

so I check to see
if my nails are dry

wonder if YouTube
could teach me

how to walk
away from them
toward myself

Before we leave

"Eden, I gotta say
what everyone's thinking:

You're fake, girl."

"What?"

Jessie and Angelica look
everywhere but at us.

"You're fake.
You act real nice.
You come here,
use my stuff,
but you don't like . . . act real."

"Real?"

"Yeah! You don't share.
You don't tell us nothing
about your life.
You know why
I'm *really* pissed at you?

I can take that
you called me out
because *whatever*

but I never saw it coming
because we don't even know you.

You want to be friends with us?
That's fine. *We're fine.*
But when you party with us
on Friday, bring the real you
or go be you somewhere else
and don't even think of coming back."

I look at the Crash

I could tell them

my mom left
Olivia dumped me
I don't even know
who that real me is

everything right now

I take my bag

go

No Part of Me Wants to Go Home

I don't know how long
I walk, only that
when my playlist ends
I'm so close to school
I decide to rest
on the playground.

I climb inside
what was once
our yellow slide,
press play on another album,
unplug my headphones,
let the music
surround me,

and send a text.

Can I ask you something?

How did you know
for sure you're queer?

It was a gut thing.

??

My gut drew me
to certain poets online.
I'd spend hours watching
strong women
hearing their words staring

I realized

I wished their words
were for me.

And then you just
came out?

Pretty much.

And everything was fine?

When I knew what I knew
I worried it would be hard
but when I finally said it
I felt freer, me-er. You know?

                                        I don't.

Hours Later

When I walk into the house
knowing I stupidly lost
track of time texting Olivia,
I think I know my fate
but I am wrong.

"Eden, you're grounded."

"What?"

"Teachers calling.
Hair dyeing.
Late arriving.
I'm done.
You run around
like you're so grown
but you're not.

Come home,
every day,
right away

or

we can find you
somewhere else to live."

And I know
with his work schedule
there's only so much time
he can keep an eye on me,
but something tells me
he means it.

OLIVIA

Rushed Hours

Every day
packed like the morning T
end to end

gathering sign-ups
helping Ms. G
cleaning tables
planning with Poetry Club
keeping up with my work?

Every day
packed like suitcases
the beginning of beginnings.

As for Eden

She texts me
more and more

I take her lead.
She shares, I listen

there's still a lot
she doesn't say

but I have to trust
she will in time.

In elementary school
I always wanted to be line leader

so now I learn at last
to take turns.

The Day Before

At our final meeting
after we run through
assigning tasks

Lexi wants us to rehearse

Elijah spits rhymes
I admit are fire

Brianna and Precious
perform as a duo
a breathless poem
on the life and loss
of their grandmother

Lexi, like always,
lifts us.

"I'm not sure this is ready."
But they make me share.

"It's ready."

The chorus of nods
(one with tears)

it's time
to make
us right.

EDEN

Friday Night I

the Crash texted all day
about this party

ding   ding   ding

each text a razor:
swift sharp

ding   ding   ding

in front of the mirror
I scrunch my curls
check the buttons on my shirt

ding   ding   ding

each a reminder
of the path I'm taking
and the path I'm not

I could turn my phone on silent
but that isn't enough

I can't spend the night
ignoring messages
about where I am / who I am
supposed to be

I leave my phone

head for the T

Friday Night II

the screech of the rails pierces
through conversations in the car

typical

if you have somewhere to go
you can count on the T
to stop you
from getting there on time

without my phone
I have no

distractions
pressure from the Crash
way to contact Olivia
sense of time

"Ladies and gentlemen,
please be advised,
we are being held between stations."

What can I do but wait?

and wait

and wait

and wait

OLIVIA

Setup

- ✓ Twinkle lights line the stage
- ✓ Preapproved playlist
- ✓ Tables rearranged
- ✓ Banner hung
- ✓ Sign in window
- ✓ Posted set list
- ✓ Mic check
- ✓ Ready

One last touch

a single daisy in a vase
on a two-person table
right by the front

a handmade *Reserved* sign

Fifteen Minutes

I read off the names
of the first five performers

look at Eden's empty table
remind myself
Fifteen minutes is a lot of time

Reread my poem
remind myself
she's coming she'll be here I know it

Five Minutes

I think about calling her
but it's loud:
her absence   the crowd   the warning

I cannot even step a toe
outside this establishment

Ms. Gonzalez would snitch,
rather Principal Z
call me down to the office than her.

Sent Not Read

You're still coming right?
Threshold Coffee? ☺

Can't wait to see you.
I have a surprise. <3

Sixty Seconds

"It's a little weird
keeping that reserved."

Lexi isn't wrong.
The manager counts
on a silent clicker, but
I swear I hear each tally
mark that she isn't here.

Even my parents stand.

"Can we hold off a little longer?
Not on starting, but on the table?"

Lexi gives my arm a squeeze.
"I'm sorry, O.
Deep breath, okay?"

Sent Not Read

Please, E?

I love you. <3

EDEN

Stuck

I stop myself from asking
for the time again

we've moved three feet
in forty-five minutes

I start to hate myself
for leaving my phone

(and try to remember . . .
did I turn it off?)

"Ladies and gentlemen, we apologize . . ."

one guy keeps
sighing loudly
as if his breath
will move
us forward

"We're being held in between stations . . ."

I try to remember
what Olivia said.

Is this event an hour?
two?

". . . due to signal problems at Stonybrook . . ."

I can't sit here
much longer
and make it
to her.

"We apologize for any inconvenience."

I can't ~~sit here~~
~~much longer~~
~~and~~ not make it
to her.

When we finally reach the next station

I won't make it
if the train gets stuck again

the conductor's story changed three times

from signal problems
to medical emergency
back to signal problems

I don't trust
the MBTA knows
the problem

mine can be solved
if I walk fast enough.

The Final Stretch

I huff and puff wind
out of my mouth
like a working train

the real train
flies by

of course

but

I can't undo my plan now,
say a silent prayer:

*To any gods listening
let me make it there
please.*

Fake Book

that's what they call
simplified versions
of famous songs
so anyone can learn them

all my life I've performed
simplified versions
of myself
so anyone can like me

tonight I shut my fake book,
decide with each step
it's time to play
the real me.

OLIVIA

While Eden's seat sits empty

Elijah gets a standing ovation

Lexi starts her performance over twice
until someone calls out

"You got this, Lexi!"
and she gets it

that's what happens
when the voices
outside your head
speak kinder than
the ones inside

at intermission
six kids ask
to join our club

all of these wins

none of them feel like it

This feels like a bad idea but

I call Eden.

A man answers.
"Hello? Who is this?
What do you want
with my daughter?"

breathless anger
car horns blaring behind

"...I..."

A sharp inhale
and he reads my texts
aloud to me, then spits,
"You don't love her.
You don't know her.
Leave her the hell alone."

I hang up
my hands shaking

I take the stage

Ask for applause

To thank Precious
for her stunning performance
To thank all our performers
To thank all our audience members
for their love and energy
and Threshold for hosting

I'm our last performer
of the night

but
before I take my last breath
to begin a poem for my love
who isn't here

the door opens
the bells attached
announce her arrival.

It is now or never

My Eden

I deliver the last lines
with closed eyes

when I open them
the crowd bursts into applause

I don't see them

I see the only person who matters

and she is there

my Eden

for

one

more

second

The bells ring again

A man barges in
grabs Eden by the arm
pulls her out

frigid wind
replaces her body

frozen
my hand still outstretched
applause fills the air

but she is gone.

Breakdown

I don't know how long I stand there

the audience saw nothing
but my performance
unsure why
I'm stuck onstage

Lexi takes me by the hand
Ms. Gonzalez gestures
to raise the house lights

and everything is too bright
so I cover my eyes
while the audience disperses
chairs scrape

Dad gives me space, Mom comes over
but I can't look at her yet

and I am sure that there is cleanup
but the Poetry Club lets me sit
head in hands

maybe for a minute
maybe forever

until no one
but Mom and I remain
and the room's silence
matches my hollowed heart.

"Let me take you home."

When the world falls out from under you II

the ground gets farther and farther away looks
    something like this:

you come home from the night   planned to recount
the tale   *I did it I won her back*
can barely make it inside   like the shoes scattered by
the front door
here seems as good a place to find ground again
and your mother   looking brighter
than she has in months   shifts to calm
secure   steady   somehow wraps her arms around
your body   like when you were small you are so
small   but you are too exhausted to help her
yourself   off the ground   she lets you rest there
for a moment

sits with you   holds your hands   tries to
remind you that this isn't you   the rightful
smoke   when a heart's fire extinguishes   a
fragile dream shaken upside down in a box marked this
side up   that this isn't you ˙ that this will not
always be you   or her

when the world falls out from under you   your heart
has a right to take the time it needs   a voice you
know but sometimes miss   surrounds you
"there will be other loves   other mistakes   both
can be true"

you close your eyes for a second

imagine your mother creates a warm glow around
you   protecting you

from holding on to now for a single second longer than
you need

you stand unsteady   let her pull you up   let your
mom's words into the space Eden left

"There will be other loves
other mistakes
both can be true."

EDEN

Away

A blur of arguments
a broken phone
a broken promise:

he is sending me away

the sound
of a piano dropped
out a window

he is sending me away

to my aunt's house in Tucson
an unmarried nurse
I've never met

he is sending me away

because
he says
I am unfixable

no one tells you what to do
when your father sends you away

On Monday morning

my father drives me to school
to clean out my locker,

plans to take me
directly to the airport

plans to leave me
there to wait, alone.

In the car, he returns my phone
but what good is it?

All contacts deleted.
All texts erased.

"This is just till you land.
Your aunt will take over from there."

I never learned her number
the only one I'd want

the only one my mind knows
now is my aunt's address.

Street View

In the Maps app
I search for my new home

study Street View
like it might tell me something.

A yellow house pressed against pixelated sky
local political lawn signs I don't know

but in a window,
a sticker with all
the rainbow colors of my heart

defines and declares to the world
my future life, a new home.

"What are you doing?"

I'm snapped back into the car,
hit the home button hard.

"Nothing,"

but a right-side-up glimmer
I keep to myself.

"Ten minutes,"

he decides, is enough
to return my books
clear out my locker

8-24-13, 8-24-13

I use my last minute
outside Ms. Gonzalez's classroom
where she spots me
signals *come in*
but I shake my head.

She opens the door.
"Eden, what's going on?"

I don't have words
for how fast
everything can change
for that moment
of leaning back, letting go.

"Can you give this to Olivia?"

Ms. Gonzalez looks at me
the folded note

until she hears a crash
from inside the classroom
spins around to quiet them

before she turns back
I go.

OLIVIA

What Healing Looks Like

in my left pocket
i carry around
eden's note
every day

carry with me
her *goodbye*
her *i love you*
her *it's okay.*

i want to believe
every word but
saw her pulled
like a ghost to a world
unknown.

in my right pocket,
i carry around
a stone from mom
to ground me

carry with me
lexi and the others saying
it's okay and *drink water*
and *breathe*

though the note's disintegrated,
first into its own creases
then blurred, faded

still, i carry a scrap of nothing
and i know i have to let it go.
but i'm not ready.
i'm not.

A few months later

after school
a postcard arrives

postmarked from Arizona
with a vast desert on the front

such emptiness in such beauty
(or such beauty in such emptiness)

and written on the back
in handwriting
I carry (even though
her note is long gone):

a web address,
a single heart,
and a letter *E*.

Composed

A YouTube channel
the avatar a keyboard
the username: Edensworld

Three songs listed
the videos are hands
nails painted for each
playing keys

a voice quietly
singing a melody
over the songs:

one for her
one for me
one for us

Origins II

My mother likes to say,
 "You came into this world
 like a poem: messy metered moments,
 fragments of possibility."

My mother likes to say,
 "You came into this world
 like a song: measured melodies,
 one listen never enough."

But now in this world,
 I live like a story: stumble through
 beginnings, middles, ends
 draft chapters past the tragedy

 so after I fall
 in, down, apart
 I'll write myself and us
 better and new.

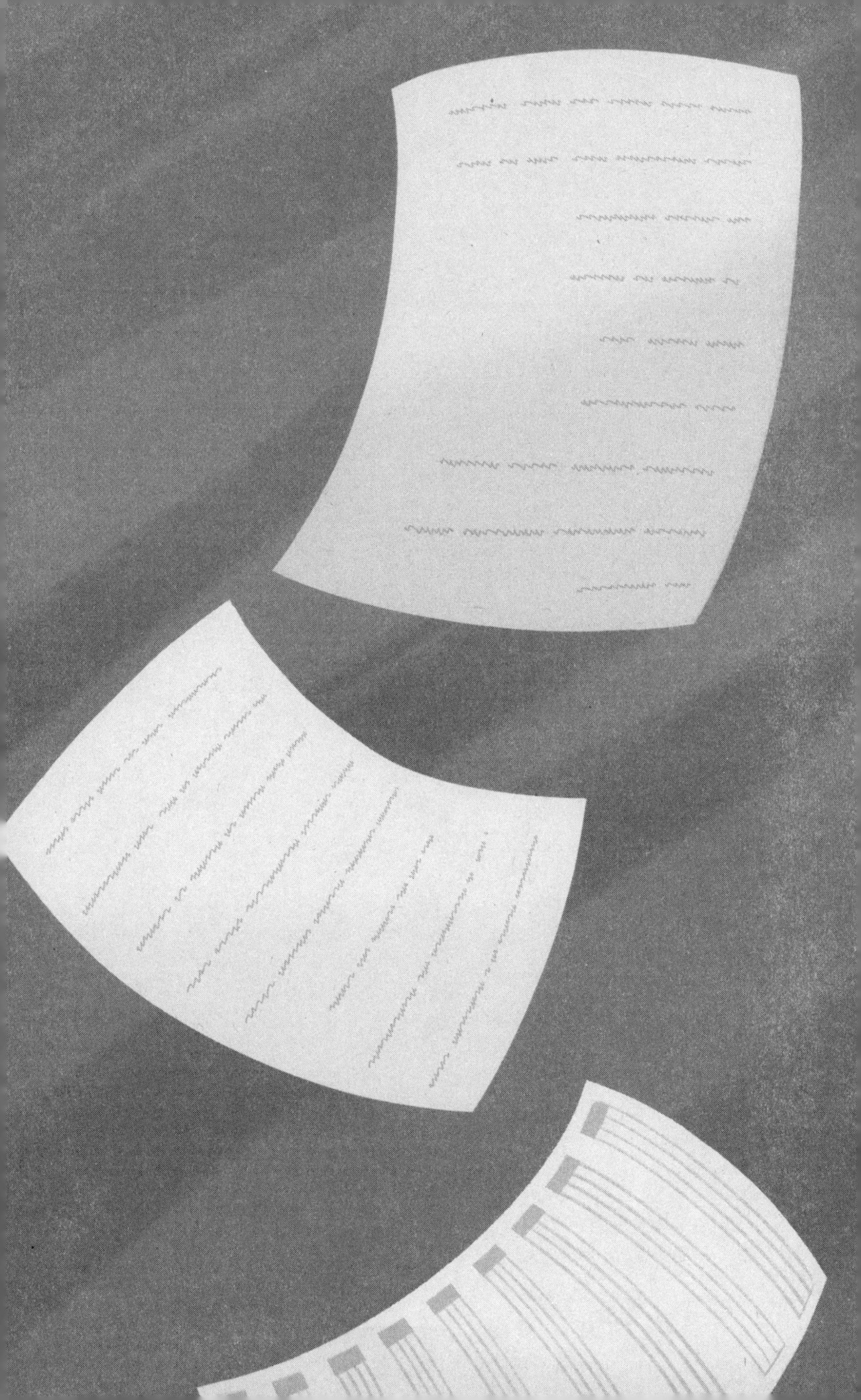

ACKNOWLEDGMENTS

I wrote this book during the pandemic, in a time when so many of us felt alone. But this book is proof I have always had the most loving community. This book is a dream made real because of the following folks and so many more.

To my agent, Eric Smith, thank you for taking a chance on me and for your tireless efforts to get Olivia and Eden out into the world. You changed my life.

This book would not be here without the expertise of the folks at Katherine Tegen Books. All my gratitude goes first to my editor, Sara Schonfeld. Insightful, communicative, generous in time and spirit, I could not ask for a better editor. Thank you to Katherine Tegen, for your feedback and for welcoming me into this wonderful imprint. For this beautiful illustrated cover, thank you to Aiyana de Vera. You brought Olivia and Eden to life in a way I never could.

Thank you also to Laura Harshberger, Jessica White, Jaime Herbeck, Kathy Lam, and Amy Ryan.

I have had a lifetime of great writing teachers, from Friends' Central to Vassar to my MFA program. I will always be grateful for Lesley University's MFA in Creative

Writing for Young People, and especially to my mentors: Cynthia Platt, for lessons in craft and heart; Michelle Knudsen, for lessons in crafting and drafting through the hardest of times; Tracey Baptiste, for lessons in precision and for making me write a new story even when I don't want to; and Jason Reynolds, for teaching me to not give up until every single page was *poetry*. How did I get so lucky to work with each of you?

To my earliest readers, Merlyn Mayhew, Valley Shaia, Bonnie McBride, and Adriana Costache, I owe my thanks. Without your enthusiasm, I'm not sure Olivia and Eden would have made it out of my drafts folder.

To my Thursday Elevators, Adria Karlsson, Rebecca Gataullin, Pata Dibinga, and Jasminne Paulino, what an incomparable gift it is to be in community with you. I can't wait to see your books in the world.

To my 2023 debut group, Ronnie Riley, Caroline Huntoon, Jen St. Jude, and Justine Pucella Winans, I am so grateful for your time, support, and good humor through all of this. Go out and buy their books, dear readers!

For your endless wisdom and friendship, thank you to Neema Avashia and Kandice Sumner. What a joy it is to have friends who are also talented writers I admire so deeply.

For constantly reminding me of the benefits of my big feelings, thank you to Nathalie Paquette.

I am forever grateful to have the world's most loving

family. To Nora Fussner, Emily Ramsey-North, and Ian Ramsey-North, you are the best siblings I could ever ask for. To my parents, Helen Rosen, Andy Fussner, and Christine Ramsey, thank you for a lifetime of encouraging me to chase my dreams.

Finally, to my wife, Clare. My number one hypewoman. My favorite person. My greatest adventure.